PAOLA CAPRIOLO was born in 19
now lives. Her first book, *La gr*
tion of short stories, won the 1988 Giuseppe Berto Prize. *Il nocchiero*, a novel, won the 1990 Rapallo Prize and in 1991 she was awarded the Förder Prize in Germany for her work. Her novels, *Vissi d'amore*, published in 1992, and *La spettatrice*, published in 1995, have both been translated by Liz Heron and published by Serpent's Tail as *Floria Tosca* and *The Woman Watching*. Paola Capriolo is also a translator, and writes for the cultural pages of *Il Corriere Della Sera*.

A MAN OF CHARACTER

PAOLA CAPRIOLO

✣

translated by Liz Heron

Funded by the Arts Council of England

Library of Congress Catalog Card Number: 99–69102

A complete catalogue record for this book can be
obtained from the British Library on request

First published in Italian as *Un uomo di carattere* in 1996
by Bompiani, Milan

This edition first published in 2000 by
Serpent's Tail, 4 Blackstock Mews, London N4 2BT

Printed in Italy by Chromo Litho Ltd

10 9 8 7 6 5 4 3 2 1

I tell myself that will must
truly be destiny because it is always
in the right against it, *hypèr móron*.

Friedrich Nietzsche

✢ **PART ONE** ✢

IN THE FINE weather, I would often end up there whenever I left the village on one of my solitary walks. Not that this place could have been described as a destination; on the contrary, to any other eyes it would have offered no attractions whatever, but somehow or other I would always wind up there. All paths seemed to lead there, or at least those I preferred, the ones that were wild and untrodden and where grass grew high among the stones and where you had to make your way by thrusting branches to one side. Along such tortuous tracks you would reach a vast hollow surrounded by hills on all sides, and only a little further on you would come across a magnificent rusty gate flanked by two pillars on which the old ornamental motifs were now barely legible. Beyond it you could just make out the old driveway, almost obliterated by weeds; wherever you looked all you could see was a tangle of greenery run riot, exactly like the thicket growing all around it.

In the distance, half hidden by the trees, a ruined villa oversaw that desolation resignedly, as if with time it had renounced all attempts to reaffirm its own dominion, nor did it have any strength left to defend itself against the assault of the creepers that made their triumphant ascent up its walls, splashing them with ragged patches of mould-discoloured green. From where I stood it was too far to distinguish these from the floral tracery decorating the facade, and the faded coat of arms, the trompe-l'oeil windows and pilasters, the closed shutters and broken listels, all of this, through neglect over time, seemed to have mutated from being something artificial into a product of nature; the human will which had constructed that building had long since retreated, leaving it a prey to hostile forces, and the result was a singular coupling of architectural and vegetable forms, a union of two opposing laws which for me exerted a deep fascination.

Sometimes I would go round the fence to the back of the house where the branches of trees, converging from both banks, fashioned a gallery above the narrow line of a gushing stream. In wet weather I could see the water swirling darkly, while in the summer it was a mere trickle slithering among the pebbles; the almost dried up river bed then gave out a faint odour of putrefaction along with the heat of the stones made molten by the sun on intermittent stretches where there was no shade.

I cannot explain why I lingered to observe all of this with such attention, filling up my pad with sketches for a painting which I could not get around to starting. Nothing there gave any hint that, only a little further on, the undulating hills would be clad in pastures, in well-kept villas and gardens, and that there would be an open perspective all the way to the blue of the lakes. But in that tangle of damp, self-enclosed vegetation there was something simultaneously disturbing and protective, almost an image of the well of chaos out of which arise the most complex expressions of life, and which finally triumphs to re-absorb them into its own indifference.

Perhaps it was just this that made it so hard to render its appearance: every mark set down by my hand on the paper seemed to express too much and too little; a secret kinship seemed to link that overflowing fullness to the void, to the empty page.

Often a botched effort could have the effect of keeping me away for days on end; then I would turn my attention to better defined objectives, to vistas more easily delineated, but the small victories I achieved were not enough to erase from my mind the sense of that great defeat. And so in the end I would go back there armed with new ideas and new hopes, with harder or softer pencils, with coarser or finer paper. I would sit on a rock not far from the fence and offer yet another challenge to the inscrutability of that place. Some hours later I would put the pencils back in their case, close my sketch pad and set out towards the village. When the landlady at the boarding house asked me if my work had gone well I would answer yes and thank her; then, in my room, I would tear out the pages I had drawn, shred them into little pieces, and throw them in the waste basket.

One afternoon, on my way up to the villa to put myself through one of these futile endeavours, I saw from a distance that the gate was ajar. The hinges, I thought, must have finally given way, cancelling out that needless frontier between the disorder on the other side of the railings and the selfsame disorder which surrounded it; the blind reach of nature, its vicious circle, seemed too far off the beaten track for me to suspect otherwise, and so I continued on my way unperturbed by curiosity. But when I reached the two tall pillars with the faded frescoes, I saw a man heading towards the villa and making heavy weather of the undergrowth. I imagined him to be a tourist more adventurous than myself, who, not content with just looking at that neglected garden, had ventured inside.

Encouraged by his example, I went through the gate and followed him, almost unconsciously assuming the respectful demeanour of a visitor to a sacred place; I was scarcely much closer, however, when I realised that the stranger's behaviour was quite the opposite. With a kind of iconoclastic frenzy, he was battering furiously at the branches with a stick so as to knock them off the tree trunks. He attacked them as if they were conscious beings endowed with reason, and his thin body was shaken by a nervous tremor. Now and then he would stop abruptly and with a brusque movement rid himself of a leaf that had settled on his hair, which was grizzled and very short, or on his immaculate town jacket, or else he would wave his free hand to drive away a cloud of midges.

Disconcerted by the strange anger with which each one of his gestures seemed to be impelled, I was on the point of moving away when he turned towards me. I nodded slightly in greeting, and he answered with a frown which gave his forehead deep furrows parallel to his eyebrows. His eyes were light coloured and cold.

He inspected me from head to toe with an alert, fastidious gaze. Finally he spoke. 'If you don't mind my saying so, your right shoelace is undone.'

Since I made no move to bend down, he smiled and

threw the stick on the ground. 'Perhaps I frightened you?'

'Not at all.'

'All the same, whatever must you have thought. Doubtless that you had come across a madman.'

I had indeed thought so, nor had I altogether given up this suspicion even now. Nonetheless, I hastened to deny it.

'Besides,' he went on, 'my response was more than justifiable. This chaos, this bedevilled place, would make anyone fly off the handle, don't you think?'

'To be honest . . .'

'Yes, you are right, hitting trees with a stick still makes no sense; there are other methods, other ways. I completely agree with you, and let me say again how deeply I regret the behaviour in which you took me by surprise.'

As he spoke, his eyes continued to inspect me in minute detail. For a few seconds they lingered over the scarf which I wore round my neck instead of a tie – a habit of mine ill thought of in those days – and I got the impression of distinct disapproval; then they rested on the sketch pad I carried under my arm.

'From what I can see, you're a painter.'

'I'm afraid you flatter me, I regard myself as a mere dilettante.'

'I see. It's just a hobby then.'

'You could call it that, if you wish.'

'And what do you do in earnest?'

I hesitated before making up my mind to tell the truth as succinctly as possible:

'Nothing.'

'Nothing? You mean, I take it, that you are still

studying for the profession which you plan to follow in the future.'

He had expressed this conjecture in such categorical tones that I felt myself obliged to confirm it. Moreover, this period in my life did indeed assume a preparatory function, even though I did not yet know what it was preparing me for. I noticed that the stranger was asking me a lot of questions without for his part feeling any obligation to tell me anything about himself; he no doubt thought that my young age gave him the right to adopt such an attitude, and to me too, I must admit, this paternally inquisitorial manner seemed quite legitimate. Despite having none of the characteristics usually associated with the idea of maturity and wisdom, in my eyes the person before me possessed an inexplicable authority.

'Pursue your studies diligently, young man. And above all, do this without ever swerving from your chosen path.'

'Always assuming,' I demurred, 'that the chosen path is the right one.'

'Ninety per cent of the time, if I may say so, the right path is simply the one followed through to the end. I could prove this to you without any trouble . . . But I'm keeping you too long, and I myself have a lot of things to do; permit me therefore to bid you goodbye.'

He held out a hand which I shook in bewilderment, astonished by this sudden leavetaking; then I turned towards the gate. A few yards away I heard the stranger's voice again: 'Don't forget to tie your shoelace.'

When I was on the track I turned round again. The

man had reached the steps which led up to the front door of the villa. He mounted them with ease, pushed the double doors wide open with a decisive movement and disappeared over the threshold.

Sometimes, rummaging among old canvases, I find myself looking at the portrait of the engineer which I painted many years ago. From memory, since he was too restless a man to sit willingly as a model, and, on those rare occasions when I managed to persuade him to pose, his physiognomy was altered almost from one moment to the next by the slightest of movements, so as to leave me with no other option but to extract from that multiplicity of contradictory images something akin to a coherent idea of the individual as I myself envisaged him.

This idea would become transformed over time, or rather, new elements would be added to the original impression, making it more complex and problematic. At the beginning I had been struck above all by the bizarre, almost grotesque aspects of his character, and I recognised their outward manifestation in that lean physique, which seemed to be made only of nerves, in the starkness of its lineaments, in the wrinkles with which his face was often marked, suddenly making him look much older than his forty years.

On the canvas I emphasised these particularities to the point of exaggeration, so that what I painted was a caricature rather than a portrait of the engineer. The lean physique was not so lean in reality, nor the wrinkles so dense and marked, nor perhaps did the features of his face possess that cruel starkness with which I endowed them. There is only one thing which I believe I rendered with complete fidelity: the posture of the body. When he stood he was as erect as a stick hammered into the ground, and even when he was sitting in an armchair I never saw him lean against the backrest or relax his arms. At any given moment his will seemed to exercise total control over all his muscles, tightening them; perhaps this is why I have never been able to imagine him asleep.

This then is the picture of the engineer which little by little took shape in my mind and then on the canvas, but after that first meeting, I retained no clear memory of him. What mattered to me was simply the conclusion to which that brief conversation had led me, namely that the villa had an owner, and the more I went over it in my mind, the harder it was for me to believe it. I had never wondered about who the garden belonged to, because it seemed natural to me that it should belong only to itself and enjoy an unchecked freedom. Now however I had to surrender to the evidence: property laws had force even over those hills and they made no allowance for land without owners.

A few days passed before I went back there. I went round the fence on the side where the stream was, and the fact that there was not a living soul to be seen made me feel an irrational relief; the stranger must have gone away, or perhaps I had misinterpreted his presence, endowing it with a significance it did not have. But in a matter of minutes a series of quick, rasping sounds, followed by prolonged creakings, brutally intervened to dispel such comforting speculations. Guided by these noises, I went up to the gate and looked through the bars. The man I had met the time before was still there, in exactly the same attitude, except for one detail: instead of the stick he was now brandishing a pruning knife of some kind and was cutting off the branches with clean well-aimed blows.

On reflection, this was not the only difference. In his behaviour there was no longer any sign of that rage which had made such an impression upon me; on the contrary, each one of his gestures appeared to be coldly calibrated so that the expenditure of energy was precisely in proportion to its end. I stood watching him for a long time without his giving any indication, absorbed as he was in his work, of being aware that he was no longer alone. He had already cleared a small stretch of ground in front of the fence. Hewn-off branches heavy with foliage were piling up at his feet, beside bundles of cut grass, as insects and lizards fled in search of a fresh refuge from which the next blow would drive them out anew.

At last he raised his head, and his look met mine. 'As you can see,' he said, after waving casually in my direction, 'I've adopted a more efficient technique.'

'Yes,' I answered, or else: 'I can see,' or something similarly vague and non-committal, and as he set about his work again I headed back towards the village. For a while, as I walked, I could still hear the rhythmic crack of the pruning knife, the creaking of the branches, and I did not stop hearing them even when the hollow was behind me. All right, I told myself, trying to suppress the anxiety aroused in me by the inexorable repetition of those sounds, I shall have to accept it now, obviously there will be someone living in the villa soon. And I made up my mind that from then on I would go up there much less often, I would choose different destinations, since that one would no longer offer me the prized charm of solitude. Luckily there was no shortage of deserted areas around the village, quiet spots where I could sit down and draw without anyone disturbing me.

But it would seem that I was lying to myself by exhibiting such indifference towards what was happening in the garden, for in the days that followed I went back there often, and each time the sound of the pruning knife would welcome me even from a distance, announcing the zealous presence of the engineer. He was still working close to the path and from time to time we would exchange a few words, though without ever embarking on a proper conversation; he made it clear he did not want to detain me, I that I did not want to divert him from his tasks, and so we were separated by a mutual reserve no less than by the railings of the fence.

All the while, with growing disquiet, I watched the deforested area grow ever wider, until one day I made up my mind to ask him if he meant to cut down many more trees.

'For now, just what is strictly necessary, what I need for breathing space. I'll soon have to go to the city, but in the meantime I'm hoping to find a good gardener, so that when I get back the work can begin on a large scale.'

I turned my eyes on the tangled waste of greenery that the engineer had heaped up against the fence. 'It would be a pity,' I said tentatively, 'to destroy everything.'

'My dear young man, it is axiomatic that without

destruction nothing can be built. Moreover, I see nothing here that merits conservation.'

'In fact, the beauty of this place is more to do with the whole than with the specific parts.'

'The beauty of this place? You are obviously fond of a joke. But why don't you come in? After all, we aren't in the visiting room of a convent or a prison, there's no one restricting us to conversation through the railings.'

'Thank you, so long as I'm not bothering you ...'

'If you were bothering me, I would not have asked you in. Anyway I was planning to give myself a little break.'

He put down the pruning knife, and, motioning me to follow him, went and sat on a plaid blanket which was carefully spread on the ground close by. I took a seat on a rock opposite him.

'Come here, I'll make room for you. I don't know what that rock is doing there, it will have to be removed.'

He sat in the middle of the blanket with his legs crossed, so as to avoid any contact with the grass, and he looked around like a general surveying the field before the battle.

'You bought this property recently, I imagine,' I said, without moving from my rock.

'I can see that next you'll be telling people I'm a madman. Buying a wilderness like this ... No, I inherited it from an uncle.'

Only then did I recall that on the first day I had noticed a black band on one sleeve of his jacket.

'Please accept my sincerest condolences.'

His face puckered up. 'Thank you, but there is no

need. I hardly knew him, I'm wearing mourning only for the sake of formalities.'

'And yet, you seem upset.'

'That's ... because of how he died.'

'I'm sorry, perhaps it was indiscreet of me.'

'There's no reason why I should make a mystery of it, but the thing is so absurd ...'

'Absurd?'

'You see, it was a chicken bone.'

'What?'

'One of those small ones, you know, a tiny little bone. My uncle swallowed it without realising.'

'I see.' My tone was regretful. 'Really bad luck.'

'Call it really absurd. However, thank heavens his death was a quick one. Now he is at peace.'

We both stopped talking for a bit, as if offering up the dutiful tribute of silence to the dear departed, and I let my gaze wander into the labyrinth of vegetation.

'I read somewhere,' I said at last, 'about an ancient Oriental teaching ...'

'About small chicken bones?'

'About the dead. According to this teaching, a month after the death, they become God, which is to say nothing.'

'I beg your pardon? What did you say?'

'That a month after the death ...'

'Yes, yes, I heard perfectly well, you don't have to take the trouble of repeating it. It's quite bad enough coming out with that kind of nonsense once, if you don't mind my saying so.

'Perhaps,' I replied in a conciliatory tone, 'if you'll let me explain better ...'

'Explain what, young man? Maybe you want to

maintain that you understand the meaning of the expression: "God, which is to say nothing"? Do you want to maintain that this expression has some generally accepted meaning?'

'A very obscure one, certainly, at least for us. I couldn't claim I understand it exactly myself, yet...'

He wasn't listening to me any more; he had got up and started attacking the bushes again. Resigned to this, I opened my sketch pad and holding it on my lap I began to copy a cluster of bushes well away from the area were he was going about his demolition work. Only after a little while did he address me again.

'What are you doing?'

'I'm drawing.'

'Yes, I can see that, but what are you drawing? Perhaps a sacred image of that God of yours who is also nothing?'

'My ambitions don't extend that far: all I'm doing is trying to sketch those bushes over there.'

He followed the direction of my eyes. 'Thank you for having drawn my attention to that piece of ugliness. I hope you won't take it amiss if I ask you to do me a favour.'

'On the contrary: whatever I can...'

'Then come and see me again, often, every time you feel like it; but leave your sketch pad at home. Let me be the one to tell you when it will be worth drawing this place.'

That evening, while I was having dinner in the boarding house dining-room, then later that night, in my room, before sleep submerged all thoughts, my mind kept going over my visit to the villa and I kept seeing the engineer attacking the trees with his pruning knife. The cold determination of his gestures, the plans which he had revealed to me only by suggestion, but which without a doubt must have been thoroughly formulated, became superimposed as a threat over the image of the garden; I would never be able to go back there, I was certain, without witnessing a desecration, nor, in any case, would I ever find there again that solitude I loved, that self-absorbed luxuriance. The very presence of the engineer, so it seemed to me then, dissipated the enchantment of the garden, or rather, deliberately rejected it. If my challenge to that place was a dedicated one, bent on reproducing its mystery, he instead had the goal of obliterating it altogether.

The garden as I knew it would thereby cease to exist. I promised myself again that I would not go back, but I would at least defend the memory I retained of it, avoiding all comparison with a different reality, and this I did, all the more sustained by the memory of the blunt, peremptory tone in which the new owner of the villa had enjoined me to leave my sketch pad at home. And yet in the days that followed I understood how much effort it would cost me to be faithful to this resolve: it was not just nostalgia, but intense curiosity which drew me there continually in thought, and I went on picturing in countless ways whatever could be happening there.

Besides, by now I had developed a lively interest in the engineer. Even his defects fascinated me, his obstinacy, the total faith in himself which shone through his every action, his every word. He was most certainly a being destined to pursue his own path right to the very end, and this aroused a kind of admiration in my irresolute nature.

I often heard him spoken of, in the boarding house or at the café, whose marble-topped tables, discoloured yellow, crammed the village square in warm weather. In fact, the local people knew no more about him than I did; indeed, their information about him was somewhat vague, probably second or third hand, since from what people said he came down to the village infrequently and stayed only as long as was strictly necessary to complete the errands which had brought him there. His shopping list displayed a decided tendency towards plain fare, bordering on frugality, and as if this were not enough, it seemed he was completely teetotal: all virtues which without doubt could not have helped endear him to the local people. By way of compensation he smoked, though not the common-or-garden tobacco sold in the village shop, but a particular variety of cigarette which was long and thin, presumably a foreign brand, which he had sent from who knows where and which he would light one after the other with a nervous click of his gold cigarette lighter. His instructions about the newspaper delivery were rigorous: every morning, copies of the principal daily newspapers had to be dispatched to reach him at seven sharp, and if his order arrived at a quarter past seven that was enough for him to threaten that he would take away his business and in future use some non-existent 'competition'.

The female section of the population regarded him with suspicion, because the new arrival was invariably absent from religious services. This omission was one which had long since been forgiven me by virtue of my being more sociable and because of my being a 'good sort', a quality which in the course of the years came to rank as an incontrovertible truth.

The engineer, on the other hand, whoever he might be, was undoubtedly not a 'good sort'; this was demonstrated by his taciturn temperament, by the haughtiness and impatience which coloured his relations with the people of the village. Often, moreover, he would ask the shopkeepers for unusual products, whose existence the former had never imagined and whose names they were not even able to repeat, however hard they might try. This combination of things made him an alien creature, a splinter detached from a different and incomprehensible world which had landed, God knows why, on their earth.

Almost in spite of myself, I paid a great deal of attention to this idle talk, eagerly seizing on the details which emerged from it. For this reason I could not describe the period when I stayed away from the villa as a true interruption in my relations with the engineer; these relations seemed rather to have assumed a latent form, and the interest I had conceived in this bizarre individual went on developing and deepening even in the absence of its object.

One morning I finally had a chance encounter at the café with this man who by now occupied such a central place in my thoughts. Although it was a splendid day, he was not sitting at one of the tables out in the square, but stood inside at the bar, gulping down a cup of tea.

As soon as he saw me he greeted me warmly. 'My dear young man, what an unexpected pleasure! Where did you disappear to, if you don't mind me asking?'

I went up to him. 'And tell me,' he continued,

without giving me time to answer, 'how are your studies progressing?'

'Quite well, thank you.'

'Well enough, I can only suppose, to leave you with no spare moments to come and see me.'

I had not imagined that he would attach any special importance to my visits, whereas he actually seemed offended.

'I was hoping to get there one of these days.'

'Good chap. Would tomorrow at five suit you?'

'Whenever you want.'

'Then let's make that definite. Now I beg you to excuse me: I would gladly stay and join you in a drink, but alas I have to run.'

He left some change on the bar counter, took the walking stick which he had left propped in the umbrella stand and left the café hurriedly.

From then on I would often go up and visit him. He did not receive me inside the house, but in that manner of artificial clearing, ever wider, which little by little he was cutting through the vegetation. All around, trees and bushes, which the late summer was already shading with brown and gold, entwined their foliage almost as if to create new hybrids and erase the boundaries between the different species, and sometimes their branches would reach out even beyond the confines of the clearing. This vegetable barrier was so intense that I often had the impression of being in a room surrounded by solid walls, and sometimes even the light failed to penetrate it, so that as soon as the rays of the sun began to fall at an angle we would find ourselves immersed in a strange twilight over which a clear bright sky would still extend.

From the very first time, the day after our meeting at the café, the engineer had equipped himself with another plaid blanket which he had stretched out next to his, and kindly but firmly he had insisted that I use it, forbidding me to sit down on the rock. That block of stone, with its jagged overhangs and its mossy crevices, aroused a deep revulsion in him: he tried hard to ignore it, anticipating its removal, and without any recourse to words he forced me to comply with this attitude.

So we sat in the clearing, conducting conversations which never touched on matters of a personal nature, or if inadvertently they made any glancing contact of the kind, there would be an immediate retreat. After a few weeks of seeing him regularly, I knew little more about him than was printed on his visiting card, which in clear plain letters bore the words: 'Erasmo Stiler, construction engineer', followed by an address in a town some distance away which had been vigorously crossed out in pen, nor did the man who answered to that colourful name take the trouble to ask me about my family or my life in town.

To make up for this we would watch one another and try to catch as much as is betrayed by the intonation of the voice, by mannerisms and preferences, and our acquaintance proceeded, gradually deepening in this indirect, almost furtive fashion. Each was for the other an individual without a past, reduced to the mobile presentness of our physiognomies, phenomena whose essence we could do no more than guess at, but not perceive.

In the course of time this individual essence would

rise ever more clearly from the magma of details, just as a statue is formed out of clay; some details would lose all importance and would move beyond the range of attention, others would take on an unexpected relevance, depending on their greater or lesser proximity to the centre of personality. From the very beginning it was clear to me that my interlocutor offered me, as a means of reaching that centre, a precious way in: if I listened to him with only half an ear whenever he talked about the weather or political events or new things in the world of art which he unfailingly deemed 'too disregarding of verisimilitude', as soon as he began sketching out his plans for the garden my interest would be re-awakened not just through the ties of affection and habit which linked me to it, but because I sensed that this was the manner in which Stiler revealed himself to me, unwittingly, much more than he would have revealed himself by telling me about his childhood or his emotional life. Even by watching him work, for instance, as he rooted out those trees and shrubs which vexed him and neatly piled up their remains in an out of the way corner, I could have reconstructed if not his biography, at least what was at the core of it.

Another illuminating clue was supplied by his style of argument: the fact was that Stiler set out his own viewpoints in cast-iron terms which were more appropriate to a scientific treatise than a simple conversation. He would often begin by saying: 'in the first place . . .' and after that first place there would follow a second, a third, sometimes even a fourth, without the count ever being lost track of, however many extremely long digressions might be interposed between one and the next. I rather envied him this capacity to keep his grip

so surely on the thread of conversation, so surely that
nothing could break it, neither my timid responses nor
even the interruptions which he was sometimes compelled to make because of his duties as a practical man;
I envied him his absolute immunity from solecism and
the ease with which he would open and close parenth-
eses, always returning to the main subject at the exact
point where he had left it. Admittedly, that crystalline
syntax, like something by a classical prose writer, produced an irresistibly comic effect when transposed into
the spoken language, so that on frequent occasions I
would find myself having to turn my face away so as
to hide my mirth; and yet, however little I was persuaded of them, it was impossible for me not to yield
to opinions maintained with such coherence, and my
mangled objections would always end up in pieces
against the indestructible wall of rigour which Stiler
unceasingly raised against any attack.

His skill at constructing periods was however combined with an extreme conciseness; first, second and
third place were usually composed of short, honed
phrases within which his thinking was condensed like
a series of definitions. This characteristic threw into
even greater relief the martial tendencies which I had
already observed in his demeanour. Stiler used words
in the same way as a strategist uses armies, aiming to
achieve the maximum result with the minimum
deployment.

In these campaigns, it goes without saying, I was the
perennial loser, and I would almost be ashamed to own
up to those ideas, in diametrical opposition to mine,
that the engineer's verbal offensives had sometimes
induced me to agree with. There was no oddity so odd

that he could not manage to sanction it with the heartiest good sense, transforming his personal likings and aversions into unimpeachable conclusions of human reasoning.

In any case, I very soon came to value those discussions, to the point where giving them up would have amounted to a severe sacrifice for me, and even when I smiled over my antagonist's victories I felt that this smile was mingled with a growing liking.

'Well then, dear Bausa,' the engineer said to me one day: this was what he called me now, simply by my surname, and each time I felt that I was back sitting in the classroom. 'Well then, dear Bausa, I will soon have to deprive myself of your company.'

'Really? I'm very sorry to hear it.'

'I think I have already mentioned to you that certain urgent business compels me to go into town. I've postponed this departure until now in the hope of being able to establish some order over my property, and especially of finding a gardener, but I cannot put off my commitments any longer. I hope to see you when I get back.'

'If the weather keeps fine I intend to stay on until the beginning of November.'

'Excellent: I shall not be away from more than ten days or so; during which time, incidentally, I shall have to find an apartment. For professional reasons I am having to move from the town where I was living.'

'So that is why you crossed out the address on your visiting card. I was sure you must have decided to settle here.'

'Here?' He cast a scornfully ironic glance at the vegetable chaos surrounding us. 'That's a peculiar idea.'

'It doesn't seem so to me. Since you inherited the villa . . .'

'Nonetheless, I could never adapt to country life; one is too exposed to the whims of the Almighty. However much one tries to adopt regular habits, something untoward always turns up, some imponderable little chicken bone, and it spoils everything. No, Bausa, man is an urban animal, he has his own natural habitat among the concrete, the asphalt, the rigorous order of straight lines.'

'Personally I feel a great sense of relief when I manage to escape from that order for a few months.'

'Because you are a romantic, your conception of nature is irremediably literary. You delight in lovely landscapes, picturesque views, and you do not discern the stupid cruelty which lies behind all this. However, even if from some crazed inner prompting I were to decide some day to move to the country, I certainly should not choose a place like this.'

'And yet, it seems to me that you have a lot of plans for this place.'

'Since it has come into my possession, albeit for reasons independent of my will, I shall clearly do everything possible to improve it; I regard it as my strict duty.'

'Your self-abnegation is truly admirable.'

'Take my word for it, I have no ambitions whatsoever for martyrdom. Simply, my mind would not be at rest, living in town, knowing that things here are not as I wish them to be. For this reason, you see, I am keen to put the garden to rights; then I will be able to entrust it to a capable pair of hands and come here only from time to time, in the summer perhaps, to reassure myself that everything is going well.'

'It could happen that you change your mind in the meantime. The seductions of the countryside are slow and stubborn; in a few months you may begin to feel their effect.'

'Nothing is impossible, dear boy, but if this were to happen I should be exceedingly surprised. You see, I am not in the habit of changing my mind.'

A few days later, when Stiler left, I found I had promised him that I would take care of the search for a gardener, and I was already regretting what had struck me at the time as a spontaneous impulse of generosity. Only subsequently, when I knew him better, did I perceive the special way he had of making use of others, asking favours with such unshakeable certainty of their being granted that he completely disarmed his interlocutors. Faced by a refusal, he would have reacted with incredulous bewilderment, as if one morning on opening the window he were to notice that the sun had failed to rise. But in this propensity to command there was nothing despotic or capricious; it originated rather in the conviction that what he wished for would always correspond to the most reasonable choice, about which no sensible person could have any cause to object.

And in fact Stiler was an incomer, while I had been visiting the village and its neighbourhood for years; he knew no one, while I knew perfectly well who to turn to. Besides, set against the countless urgent commitments with which he had to contend even in summer, there was my status of holidaymaker, free to make whatever use I pleased of my time.

So I set about finding a gardener who would have all the qualities scrupulously listed by Stiler on delegating this task to me. In the first place, the candidate would have to agree to live in one of the villa's annexes. The fact that the villa did not have any annex whatsoever was a negligible drawback in the eyes of the engineer: the annex would be there, when the time came, a simple but seemly little dwelling, equipped with every necessary convenience. The second requirement was that the man should have neither children nor pets, categories for which the new owner maintained a marked aversion; this requirement would however have to be reconciled with a third, namely that the gardener should be married: what was needed was a woman in a position to get the household chores done, but God forbid, not in a position to reproduce. In short, it was a matter of finding a couple on their own, no longer young and willing to move house.

After a few fruitless inquiries among people of my acquaintance, I handed the task over to the landlady of the boarding house, and the latter, after having sung their praises at length, introduced me to distant relatives who in age and matrimonial state corresponded to the engineer's directions. He was a corpulent man, she a dried-up little woman. He never talked, she hardly ever stopped. It was the woman in fact who told me, complainingly, that her husband had for years devoted his energies to looking after a public park in a nearby town until the local Council, under the pretext of his having reached the maximum legal age, had discarded him 'like an old shoe'. Since then the two of them had lived, or rather struggled to make ends meet, on a pension which the rising cost of living made increasingly inadequate.

Since, notwithstanding their unswerving dedication to this end, the Lord had never seen fit to bless them with a child, they found themselves compelled to face the rigours of old age alone, something which had not yet managed to impair the robust hard-working fibre of which they were made; so if the engineer, Mr Stiler, were to decide to take them into his employ, he would be doing a good deed and at one and the same time striking a bargain which was very much in his favour.

The presentation of this plea turned out to be intolerably long-winded, but the information I extracted from it seemed satisfactory. Stiler had left me the number of his hotel, and that same evening I rang him from the public telephone booth to tell him that everything had been settled perfectly well.

'Good, let's hope so,' he said, his voice distant across the static. 'My thanks for the trouble you have taken.'

'Not at all, no trouble.'

'Obviously, however, before employing them I shall have to have a look at their background. Did they show you any references?'

'They're local people, well thought of in the village. They have never been in service.'

'But does he know anything about gardening?'

'He worked in a public park.'

'It means nothing, dear Bausa, it means nothing. Don't take it any further for now: I'll be back on Thursday, then I'll be able to speak to him personally.'

Thus on the Friday morning the would-be gardener was summoned to the villa and put through stringent questioning, of whose outcome Stiler informed me that very day.

'Unfortunately, this person is very far from

possessing the necessary competence, with those vague, superficial notions he has.'

'I thought that his long experience . . .'

'When principles are erroneous or deficient, experience can only serve to perpetuate the error. For example, on the subject of fertilisers your protégé expressed views that were doubtful, to say the least.'

'I'm really sorry.'

'No, no, you are not to blame, in fact, I want to thank you again for your interest; I realise, however, that it would be better for me to take care of this matter myself. I shall have to stay on here for a while, which is no bad thing; since in town I achieved nothing.'

'You haven't found an apartment?'

'Not yet. I wanted to visit some relatives of mine who live there and ask them to help me look for one, but I didn't even find them at home; they are probably on holiday somewhere. As you see, Bausa, luck refuses to come to my aid.'

Stiler had promised to let me know as soon as he found a gardener, but many days went by without any news reaching me, and meanwhile, as autumn drew on, the time was approaching when I would have to leave the village and go home again. On the eve of my departure I decided to go and say goodbye to the engineer and I walked there along the shortest of the paths leading up to his property. I expected still to find, as on earlier occasions, something of that wild place I had known, but when I reached the gate what met my eyes was an expanse of almost totally bare ground at the centre of which the villa displayed its own re-conquered supremacy. In place of the creepers, scaffolding planks ran along the walls, and here and there, tiny in the distance, could be discerned the figure of a man intent on renovation work. All that was left of the erstwhile vegetation were two age-old oaks and a handful of other trees with yellowing leaves.

In the distance I saw Stiler striding about the grounds and using the tip of his stick to outline what seemed to be a vast geometric pattern, studding it with crosses which he arranged in strict symmetry. Each of these gestures was followed by a brief exchange of words with the man walking beside him, a sturdy fellow, getting on in years, and the latter would answer with repeated nods of the head to indicate his own assent.

When I reached them and the owner of the house introduced the new gardener to me I recognised the person whom I had suggested and Stiler had rejected because of his lack of competence.

'It's a stopgap,' he explained to me once we were alone. 'He's the best I can do here, and I was pressed to get the work started. You know, I have to leave tomorrow.'

'What a coincidence: I came to say goodbye to you.'

'You too are going back to town?'

'Tomorrow morning, on the eleven o'clock train.'

'The eleven o'clock train . . . Yes, that suits me perfectly. If you have no objection, we can travel together.'

'It will be a pleasure.'

'However, I must ask you to get the tickets, because I'll have a lot to do in the day ahead. That's really kind of you,' he went on, hardly leaving me time to give my agreement. 'We'll meet at the station, ten minutes before departure.'

'Until tomorrow then; I'll be off now, I don't want to keep you from your tasks.'

'At least let me offer you a cup of tea.' He glanced at his watch. 'It's still early, I can allow myself a twenty minute break.'

I followed him, trying as much as possible not to look around as we crossed the garden, over which a premature and extraordinarily severe winter seemed to have fallen. Stiler had never made any secret of his intentions, yet I had not expected to see them enacted in such drastic fashion. I recalled trees which I had thought would be spared, certain spots which were worthy of more merciful treatment; but the engineer, faithful to his principles, had carried out the project of annihilation quite thoroughly without ever swerving from the path upon which he had begun, and now, in the cold morning light, he trod that bleak expanse with the arrogant step of the victor.

At last we entered the house. Of the internal walls only the masonry remained and the upper floor was visible through the beams that once had supported the ceiling. The scaffolding nets blanked out the windows and light entered only from above, through the dormer windows, like rays descending from the dome of a church.

'This house is reduced to a shell,' said Stiler shaking his head, 'I'll have to re-build it almost from scratch. You know, my uncle lived abroad, and I don't think he ever bothered to come here to check the state of the property.'

'What was his profession?'

'He was an engineer, like me. He designed bridges for the big rivers in the north: immaculate projects, downright technical masterpieces. Until the little chicken bone . . .'

'You torture yourself too much.'

'I don't torture myself at all, I've already told you that my uncle never meant very much to me. It's just that the episode in question strikes my sense of aesthetics as intolerable.'

'I fear that death is always anti-aesthetic.'

'On the contrary, it can and should be the natural crowning of a life, enacted in harmony with the laws which govern it. We should die of what we lived by so that death does not become an outrageous absurdity. For example, think of the soldier fallen on the battlefield.'

'An example which is hard to emulate in peacetime.'

'Pardon me, dear Bausa, but I'm compelled to contradict you once again. If my uncle had been killed by the collapse of a bridge he was building . . .'

'He would have shown himself to have been an extremely bad engineer.'

'Well then, at least he would have died of being an extremely bad engineer and not in that arbitrary way which could happen to anyone. Is going to university perhaps a requirement for swallowing a chicken bone? Come now, please, take a seat: my twenty minutes have gone down to ten.'

In one corner of that great desolate room a little wicker table and some easy chairs had been arranged, garden furniture doubtless left behind by the former owner, and made grotesque by their smallness in that interior. As soon as we had sat down, the gardener's wife came to serve us with tea. I have no idea where she could have made it: looking around I saw no other furniture, and there were no walls to mark off any space that could have been used as a kitchen. Moreover I was wondering where the engineer could have slept all this time, but as I have already said I never managed to persuade myself that he really did sleep.

Now he watched the thin figure of the servant as she left, a look of satisfaction in his eyes. 'As for future progeny,' he remarked in a low voice, lighting a cigarette, 'I think my mind can be at rest.'

'Quite. The woman must be fifty at least.'

'Even if she were younger . . . You see, I flatter myself that I have a deep understanding of human beings, that I can pigeonhole people according to type, and that type takes more pleasure in talking about other people's lives than in living their own.'

'An annoying habit.'

He shrugged. 'Being here, she won't have many opportunities to cultivate it.'

This reference the engineer made to his solitude struck me, not because it revealed something unexpected, but because it confirmed what I had guessed at for some time without actually being aware of it: after all, it could be that I too was endowed with a deep understanding of human beings. Stiler subdivided them into types, probably designating each type with a precise name and establishing exactly those characteristics which each specimen had to display in order to be so assigned; my own knowledge proceeded more by experience, along more instinctive lines. Thus I did not know to which type the person sitting opposite me belonged, but I was certain that I was unlikely ever to see him in the company of a woman or surrounded by a gang of friends.

Even the place upon which he had chosen to unleash his powers of control seemed to me then to be deeply foreign to his being, as if between him and that margin of nature there prevailed a reciprocal non-belonging or even a mutual hostility. Perhaps this is the reason why I did not draw him in the garden, but against a uniform background of brown earth: to have created a different setting for him would have struck me as a falsification.

The next morning, the landlady of the boarding house bade me an emotional goodbye on the threshold and made me promise as she did every year that I would return the following spring, and as she did every year she instructed her son to take me and my luggage in the gig to catch the train. In keeping with an old custom of my own, I had left something in the chest of drawers, a scarf to be precise: this was a ritual which I enacted always at the moment of departure in order to favour my return, or, if you like, a pledge of fidelity which I gave to the village. I knew that it would be taken care of, and that in the spring I would find it waiting for me in the same place where I had left it.

When we got to the station, I asked the boy to unload the luggage and then I dismissed him with a good tip. After buying the tickets I sat down on a bench facing the tracks to wait for my travelling companion. I looked at the squat pink building flanked by two well-kept flower-beds, and at the houses which made tentative forays up the lower slopes of the thickly wooded hills, and I wished myself already on the train so as to escape that state of melancholy suspension.

Meanwhile the time for departure was approaching.

I did not doubt that Stiler was a punctual individual, with a pathological punctuality where time was the object of the same obsession with order and precision which marked his attitude towards space; therefore, when at ten to eleven I saw no sign of him, I began to worry, and another five minutes later I was seriously concerned.

Just as the bell rang to signal the arrival of my train, I observed the gardener heading towards me breathlessly.

'The engineer is sorry,' he told me, after walking the length of the platform while keeping well clear of the tracks, 'but he can't come.'

'Has something happened? Is he unwell?'

'No, sir, he's very well. I've got a note for you here.'

Hearing the whistle of the locomotive, I slipped the envelope which he held out to me into my pocket and hurriedly picked up my luggage. I had scarcely time to get into the carriage. Once I was sitting in the first empty compartment I managed to find, I unsealed the envelope and read the note:

Dear Bausa,

I regret having caused you so much trouble for nothing. The pressing requirements of work on the garden compel me alas to postpone my departure, depriving me of the pleasure of travelling with you. As soon as I'm in town, which is to say a week from now at the latest, I shall take the liberty of telephoning you; in the meantime please accept my best wishes.

Yours,

Erasmo Stiler

I did not find this sudden change of plans in any

way out of the ordinary, even though it ill matched the idea I had formed of the engineer as a man who was steadfast in his decisions. On the other hand, he was also a man who never left things half done, and I therefore even judged it perfectly natural that he should have decided not to leave before having organised everything down to the last detail.

I put the note back in the envelope and looked out of the window. The train, proceeding at speed, had already left behind the last houses in the village, and the high ground began to dip gently towards the plain.

If I think back over that winter, I can only view it as a void whose real meaning lay outside it in the different seasons it foreshadowed, when I would be back in the village and would see the engineer again: but in reality he had not yet become so important to me as he appears in retrospect, and after just a few weeks I gave up waiting to hear from him. I certainly had never imagined that this acquaintance would develop into a deep bond, of the kind to last a lifetime, and even less would I have imagined that one day I would be moved to write these pages in order to establish in some way a picture of Erasmo Stiler, his fate and the role assigned to me in its enactment, with such scrupulous tenacity, as if fearing lest I should see a fundamental part of my own existence slip through my fingers.

No, I had no inkling of all this, and yet even then, whenever I remembered the engineer, I realised the special value of this remembering, which distinguished it quite sharply from how one recalls assorted persons with whom ephemeral relationships are made on holiday and are incapable of outlasting a change of scene. Unlike these, the image of Stiler lived on, perhaps because it often happened that I would compare myself with him, as a comparison is made between one thing and its opposite in order better to discern its nature.

I thought back to our first meeting and I wondered whether he had been able to discern a hint of pride in my voice when I had described myself as a mere dilettante: the awareness of being only an onlooker at the millenarian conversation between works of genius, with no hope of participating, did not humble me in the least; on the contrary, it had a reassuring effect, since to it was linked the precious freedom, which I would never have wished to give up, to immerse myself completely in contemplation.

All that poets, painters and musicians had laboured to create over the centuries lay before me like an endless festive banquet from which I could taste, free from all care, first one, then another dish, and even painting was for me just a different manner of observing. This probably accounted for that absence of style of which my friends accused my paintings: it was the search for a position of neutrality which allowed me to take and give back the imprint of objects without falsification. Yet even in this search my will was not totally involved; instead, I kept myself in a mental state of disinterested receptivity, being attentive to impressions and almost indifferent to the outcome. This deep-seated outlook gave me the certainty which I had always had, that my life would run its course safe from all that is ridiculous, but also what is tragic and sometimes great, in every failed ambition.

And it is perhaps here too that Stiler's friendship had

its origin, that strange friendship, lacking in warmth, which as it grew and became firm would never reach a point where the membrane of reserve in which it had been enclosed from the start would ever be broken. What made us so precious to one another was that very antithesis of our natures: just as I needed images to hold in my consciousness, so he would have sought and found in me a smooth surface to reflect his actions and send him back their meaning.

In the city it seldom happened that I was able to spend time drawing, but occasionally I snatched a few hours for my favourite occupation and would sit at the little table with a lamp as substitute for the miserly sun of the winter afternoons. It was often my intention to draw the garden, to make it come alive again at least on paper, but this idea never worked for me, not even in the approximate state which I had managed to achieve the summer before. Gradually I became aware that it was no longer in my power to make a representation of that place as it had once been; all that came into my mind, with a savage persistence, was the expanse of almost bare ground upon which lines and crosses formed symmetrical patterns.

The first March sunshine rekindled my desire for the countryside. New grass had already covered the flower-beds in the city parks with a gloss of green which had something fragile in its splendour, and I felt an impulse to leave at once for the village and catch that brief season, that fullness of life destined to ebb with every day that passed, into an ever more impoverished economy of energies; but since my studies still required my presence in town, it was only at the end of May that I could finally allow myself a holiday on the sole condition which I find acceptable, in other words without having to fix its ending in advance, so I took the train to the village, leaving unresolved, even in my own mind, whether my stay would last only weeks or be prolonged into the autumn.

Through the train window I watched the landscape's gradual alterations, the industrial suburbs, in those days not extensive, almost immediately making way for the vast openness of the plain, and then its rising undulations where fields and woods alternated with a rhythm which seemed devised to offer a pleasing variety to the eyes of the traveller. Every now and then along that familiar route I would observe some detail which I had already noticed on other occasions and adopted as a landmark in order to judge the distance from my destination: a church, a bridge, a farm, the ruins of a castle on a hilltop, signs which now, on the outward journey, inverted the meaning they had whenever I returned, and from being melancholy signals of city life were transformed into ever more explicit hints of the happy idleness which awaited me in the village.

From the very first day, after taking possession of my room and having ascertained with gratitude that the scarf was still in the chest of drawers, I should have liked to go up and see the engineer, but given that he had not been in touch again, I feared that a visit on my part might cause his displeasure, and besides I felt obliged to make a show of a resentment which I did not harbour towards him in reality.

As I learned from the landlady of the boarding house, Stiler had spent the whole winter at the secluded villa, which had been almost cut off by the snow, and had come down to the village very rarely. In people's eyes he had become a figure now clothed in an aura of legend, but when they referred to him each of them assumed that mocking tone in which ordinary people usually speak of what they do not understand, and which perhaps would disturb them if they could not raise a smile at it. They spoke of the engineer as 'the hermit', a peculiar fellow not to be taken too seriously.

Yet there was no one who had failed to observe with interest the comings and goings of vans laden with bricks and gravel, then furniture and finally, at the beginning of spring, with plants packed close together, their roots protected by a white paper wrapping printed with the name of some nursery a long way away. Nearly every day one of these went by, stopping momentarily in the square, where the driver would get out to ask directions, then disappearing into the hills, and after a complicated stretch of driving it would climb up along one of my favourite tracks, now asphalted and employed as the access road to the villa.

All of this, together with the stories told by the gardener's wife, who maintained an amphibious position between the two worlds, by virtue of her frequent trips to the village, conjured the hermit's retreat as an enormous hive in whose industrious atmosphere the raw materials transported by the trucks were converted into solid form, like honey from nectar.

Whether out of inertia or because they shied uneasily away from this man who remained an outsider after months in residence, the local people avoided Stiler's property, and there were very few who could say that they had gone up as far as the gate even once; but the garden, around which the hills cast their protective embrace as if to defend it from alien eyes, was the subject of marvellous tales, and in descriptions which were either purely invented, or else the fruit of some freely fabricated fancies grafted onto scant concrete details, this once wild, forgotten place grew in opulence and size to the point where it was transmuted into a manner of Versailles.

Now they referred to the engineer's villa with pride, as if it were a monument whose lustre was shed across the whole area, yet they continued to regard its architect with amused irony, relegating to the Hades of incomprehension that comical Titan who lit his fires beyond the hills.

I had been in the village already for several days, and I had had my fill of listening to the country people's fantasies, when one morning, as I was finishing breakfast in my room, I heard a knock on the door.

'Who is it?'

'It's Ursula, sir.'

'Ursula?'

'Mr Stiler's maid.'

She entered the room in response to my invitation, and after greeting me began looking around eagerly, as if to register every detail that was presented to her eyes. As soon as she came near my table I ostentatiously closed the sketch pad which I had left open there the night before, but she seemed to take no notice whatsoever of that implicit reproof.

'You haven't forgotten about us, have you, sir? Of course, it's been some time now, and there may have been a lot of distractions down there in the city, a lot of new acquaintances...'

'I remember you very well.'

'So much the better. And you surely haven't forgotten my master either, even though you haven't come to see us up at the villa yet since you've been back. I'm not saying so as a criticism, I wouldn't dare, nor has the engineer, I can assure you, ever said anything of the kind. He just instructed me to deliver this letter to you.'

She handed me an envelope, and I opened it at once. Under the maid's alert gaze, which seemed to want to decipher what was written on the paper by studying my face, I read the 'letter', which consisted of a single sentence: 'When do you intend to honour me with a visit?'

'Tell him that I shall be there tomorrow. No, instead, this very day.'

'Good, sir, come whenever you wish: it's not as if you are likely to find him out.'

This remark, voiced with a little smile of complicity, was obviously meant to preface a detailed account of the engineer's habits. I hesitated, torn between discretion and the desire to learn something more about Stiler than what he himself would be willing to reveal to me. In the end the second of these sentiments prevailed.

'Does your master,' I asked, 'lead a very secluded life?'

'He certainly does: the only difference now between him and a hermit is that he's got no cave. And of course the fact that he still smokes like a Turk. Hermits don't usually smoke, do they, sir? Anyway, he hardly sets foot outside the gate any more; he's so busy with that garden of his ... he can't think about anything else. You see, that's why I breathed a sigh of relief when they told me that you'd come back to the village, and I breathed another one this morning, when the engineer gave me the letter. It will do him good to talk to somebody, being on his own he gets more peculiar every day, harsher.'

'Harsher?'

'Yes, sir. For that matter, he must always have been harsh, it'll be in his nature.'

'He's unkind to you, is that it?'

'It's not that, sir. Sometimes his manner is a bit brusque, no denying that, but we are used to it, we don't even notice it. There are a lot of things you have to put up with when you have the misfortune to be born poor, and to stay that way into the bargain.'

'All the same, that's not it?'

'No, sir; what I really can't stomach is his cruelty, his lack of love and respect for God's creatures.'

I thought I understood what she was referring to. 'Nor was I, I can assure you, at all happy about him cutting down all those trees.'

'If he'd gone no further than the trees, it wouldn't matter so much; whereas... Um, you'll see for yourself.'

'I'll see what, Ursula?'

'Anything that isn't the way he wants it to be has to disappear, no mercy, it has to be wiped off the face of the earth. Do you honestly think, sir, does this seem to you how a Christian should behave?'

'Still, I don't believe the engineer is a cruel man.'

'Who knows. I admit that sometimes I even feel sorry for him, and then I wonder where his obstinacy will lead him.'

'I too sometimes wonder. But tell me, how is the garden getting on?'

'Come and see it for yourself. It's something that can't be described, a wonder. But . . .'

'But . . .?'

'You'll notice it without my telling you, I don't want to say a word. What's certain is that you'll have trouble recognising it; it is so different from when you last saw it . . . There is no denying that the engineer has been able to achieve miracles, in such a short time.'

'Well, this afternoon I can be my own judge. Thank you for now, Ursula, and please accept, for your trouble . . .'

'No trouble, sir is too kind,' said the servant, hurriedly pocketing the tip I handed to her. 'Though it is true, at my age, to keep on going up and down that blessed road, from the villa to the village, from the village to the villa . . . But what can you do, we are born to suffer and we just have to resign ourselves to the inevitable. Oh, I almost forgot: Mr Stiler gave me another message for you. It occurred to him after he'd sealed the envelope, and so . . .'

'What message is that?'

'He says that now, if you want, you can bring your sketch pad and pencils.'

However much I tried to distract myself by drawing, the morning went by with unusual slowness; the talk in the village had aroused my curiosity to such an extent that every day, before receiving that laconic invitation, curt as an order, I had had to exercise considerable restraint in order to stop myself from going up to the villa, and now my impatience had been intensified by Ursula's words.

At what struck me as a suitable point in the afternoon I finally left the boarding house, and after crossing the village, then a good stretch of countryside, I turned onto the steep asphalted road. The sun was still high, the sky clear, and everything seemed singularly distinct, as if a painstaking artist had taken meticulous care over every branch, every blade of grass. When I reached the hollow I found myself in front of a high boundary wall, broken exactly in the middle by a gleaming gate which seemed intent on denying any kinship whatsoever with its rusty predecessor.

To one side of the gate I saw an electric bell, yet I did not ring immediately, but paused to observe what I could make out of that now unrecognisable place through the bars. With the determination of someone who has no time to waste, a straight gravel driveway led up to the main entrance of the villa, which had been re-painted with a thick covering of white that completely obliterated the floral ornaments and the trompe-l'oeil pilasters; only the coat of arms had been spared, and in the re-found brilliance of its colours it stood out against the snowy background. I observed the new windows with their shining glass, the shutters without a listel out of place; this renovation was so scrupulous that it had stripped the building of its past, and what little could still be felt of its primitive style of architecture was not enough to flaw the sense of modernity which emanated from the whole. From this position I could not see much of the garden, though enough to realise that everything presented to the gaze on one side of the drive: hedges, shrubs, flower-beds with blooms which drew neatly outlined patterns against the shorn grass, was repeated on the other side of it with unfailing symmetry.

I was on the point of ringing when Stiler came towards me. He seemed rejuvenated, and the nervosity of his movements had given way to a more balanced demeanour, a certain subdued vigour.

He opened the gate with a joyous impatience which was unexpected.

'I find you well,' I said shaking his hand.

'Thank you, I too find you very well. But don't keep me on tenterhooks, tell me what you think of it right now.' And the broad sweep of his arm encompassed the whole garden.

'I think . . . that you have left nothing to chance.'

A gleam of satisfaction came into his eyes. 'That is exactly what I wanted to do. You know, I was so eager to show the fruit of my labours to someone who would be able to appreciate it . . . But you have seen nothing yet, I can assure you: the beauty of the garden, as I planned it, can only be grasped through a detailed inspection. If climbing up here hasn't tired you out . . .'

'Not at all.'

'Then come with me: I'll be your guide.'

The details, which he pointed out to me one after the other, reinforced the icy impression made by the whole. Hedges and shrubs had been trimmed and had taken on spherical, conical, and parallelpiped forms, as if the engineer had inculcated Euclid's postulates into the very heart of organic nature. He clearly preferred things that grew in modest dimensions, perhaps for their greater docility; only the two age-old oaks saved from the destruction spread vast circles of shadow upon the tender grass, and with their equidistance from the villa they demonstrated this to be the ideal centre of the little universe.

Sometimes my host bent to pull out some surreptitiously grown weed and threatened severe measures against the gardener, or he would stop and inspect a plant with a critical look, half closing his eyes with the mien of a painter inspecting a picture to check that each of its parts is in harmony with the whole. Instead of standing up straight like its companions, one of the flowers arranged in compact rows to form the border of a flower-bed drooped its corolla so that it rested on the gravel. Stiler straightened it at once, propping it up with a twig.

'It's a battle, you see, a perpetual battle. Which means that you have to keep an eye on every inch of ground and examine it day after day.'

For a few moments he stood still, a worried stare fixed on the wild vegetation which pushed forward right up to the edges of the property; then he moved on again, and I followed him.

As I got close to one of the oaks I remarked that beneath its canopy, as doubtless beneath that of its twin, a small stone table had been set, surrounded by some chairs. With their bases fixed into the ground all of these were unmovable.

'It's my custom to have tea here, at five on the dot. You'll come and join me often, I hope.'

When we went back along the pathway, the indolent flower was lying on the gravel again, and with a decisive gesture Stiler uprooted it. 'You must admit, Bausa, I had been lenient. I had given it a chance to mend its ways: the fault is its own for not making the most of it.'

We reached the back of the house, where the stream once meandered. Somehow or other, the engineer had managed to dam the flow and now in its place there ran a canal which, after describing a curve, proceeded along one side of the villa, opening out into a small artificial lake which was perfectly round and whose centre was marked by a group of water lilies. With an almost theatrical instinct for building up effects, the last thing he showed me was undoubtedly what he regarded as his masterpiece. I admired it, and yet I could not stop myself from bringing to mind the winding stone-studded river bed with its sinuous streaming rivulets and the foliage-laden branches which reached from one bank to the other until they touched.

I thought back on the words of the maid, and again I refused to give them credence. No, the engineer was not a harsh man: he had merely sworn a mortal hatred of disorder, of the random, of chicken bones. With a rigour in which I was compelled to recognise a certain grandeur, he had banished all of this from his land, transforming it into a triumph of confines and calculation.

It took me some time to find any charm in the cold beauty of the garden, and even more time to understand that it was not just a matter of beauty; this judicious arrangement of forms, in which Stiler perceived the pure visible assertion of his will, breathed and lived through an element which was not visible, not willed, and which it unceasingly evoked as opposites evoke one another. Thus the sunniest and most harmonious works of art often acquire a disturbing fascination when

we begin to sense the dark fundament from which
they safeguard us with their play of limpid proportions,
when we recognise in them the sentinels posted to
defend a dangerous frontier.

In contravention of Stiler's express wish, I never
brought my sketch book and pencils with me, nor did
he ask me again to do so, but I am convinced that he
felt some faint resentment. My refusal to draw the new
garden must have struck him as a sign of half-hearted-
ness towards his offspring, or worse still, a secret
partisanship towards the defeated enemy, and in fact it
was perhaps both of these things; but what held me
back above all was my awareness of a deep alienation.
That place was irreconcilable with my nature; of course,
I could have made a few sketches without encountering
too many problems, without even feeling that sense of
impotence which the garden of the past had so often
provoked, and in this way I would have made the
engineer happy. Yet it would have been like making a
faithful copy, while taking pains to avoid spelling mis-
takes, of a page written in a language which I did not
understand.

Besides, I don't believe that Stiler had time to let this
grieve him too much, busy as he was defending his
creation from the continuous assaults of rebel forces.
To me the garden seemed completely tamed, an animal
restrained by a humiliating captivity, but the engineer
was very far from sharing this opinion; as he put it,
the vegetation exhibited an uncontrollable tendency to
escape the rigid designs which he had imposed on it,
and their preservation required constant vigilance; the

hills, with their unruly luxuriance, literally laid siege to the garden, and the capricious conduct of atmospheric phenomena always gave him fresh cause for worry. But his indignation was aroused most of all by the birds, whose voracity, as he would state in a tone which left no room for dispute, represented a grave threat to plants and trees.

One day, as I was going through the gate of the villa, I heard the sound of gunfire. Ursula ran towards me waving her arms about wildly. 'Oh sir, what I have to be witness to! Didn't I tell you that he's cruel, that he has no compassion for God's creatures!'

I saw the engineer in the distance. He had a rifle slung over his shoulder and was staring at the clear sky with a challenging look.

'What was he firing at?'

'The birds, sir, those poor innocent things that come here in search of some food. There has to be a reprisal, that's what he said, an exemplary punishment: kill two or three of them and the rest will learn to keep well away.'

'And did he hit any?'

'I don't know, sir. All I saw was a great beating of wings up there. Look at him, how pleased with himself he looks, as if he'd done something to be proud of! A demon, that's what he is.'

I joined the engineer. 'Well, dear Bausa,' he said as soon as he saw me, '*you*'re not going to come and tell me I'm bloodthirsty. I've already explained to you, I'm living under a state of siege and all I can do is defend myself.'

On the ground, at his feet, lay the small body of a sparrow, motionless, its wings stiffened.

'Come now, young man: if the sight of this upsets you, there is no reason for you to stand there looking at it so obstinately. There is something morbid in your pity, if I may say so, and something excessive too.'

At that moment I really did not like him, yet I followed him without a word in reply. We sat down at one of the little stone tables and he called the maid.

'Sir?'

'It's teatime, if I'm not mistaken.'

'Certainly, I'll see to it right away,' she answered acidly. 'It's been a tiring afternoon, sir will be in need of refreshment.'

She returned shortly, bringing the tea, and served it gracelessly. Clearly the fact that I remained silent transformed me in her eyes into the engineer's accomplice.

'It has to be acknowledged,' he said when Ursula had gone, 'that the woman has a mind of her own, I'll have to put up with being in the wrong for a while. You see, dear Bausa, the difficult situation in which I find myself? All I needed was civil war.'

'Stop shooting the birds and peace will be reestablished before long.'

'Well done, a really excellent piece of advice. Let them all have their way for the sake of peace: the birds, the half-witted old servants . . .'

'If you were to grant Ursula her wish, perhaps the garden too would derive some benefit from it. The birds feed on insects and larvae, they see to it that parasites are got rid of; their usefulness is undoubtedly greater than the damage they cause.'

'No one will ever succeed in convincing me that two disorders can produce a state of order. But I did not know I had the honour of talking to an expert in agriculture.'

'Staying in the country so often . . .'

'You consider that you've learned something? That could be, yet your conception of nature is still purely sentimental, and believe me, sentimentality does not take you far. You are a painter, so you ought to know how much coldness is a pre-requisite for achieving the goal you set yourself.'

'I've told you, I'm just a dilettante.'

'Perhaps because you have not yet learned to hold your impulses in check. I too lay some claim to having extended my knowledge in recent months, and not only with regard to methods of cultivation.'

'I heard that you stayed here all the time.'

'I had to. Putting the garden to rights required a constant commitment, I would hazard to say a total dedication, and the same thing is required to keep it as you see it.'

'So do you intend to put this address on your visiting card?'

He did not even hear me. He was looking up, and when I raised my own eyes I saw a small flock of birds crossing the sky.

'There they are coming back; the lesson was not enough, it seems.' He got up, slung his rifle over his shoulder again, and after taking accurate aim he fired into the air to put the enemy horde to flight.

My knowledge of Stiler and of the new garden deepened in parallel during the weeks which followed, and there was nothing that I discovered in the one which I was unable to find some trace of in the other. And yet, not even now was this place altogether in harmony with its maker as being his natural environment; probably Stiler did not feel at home in what he described as his own artifact. They mirrored one another, but this precisely presupposed a distance, the same distance which became intolerable to Narcissus when he contemplated his own image in the fountain and recognised the futile fleeting contact of two twin solitudes.

Thus the engineer remained in my eyes as a figure without a background, and the garden, notwithstanding the domestic rituals celebrated in it daily, continued to be an uninhabited landscape. The rigour with which it had been conceived and created seemed to rule out the possibility that any living being, its owner included, could really have a place there, that a life based on movement could be reconciled with the fixity of its forms. Even the flowers, the plants, the leaves, seemed as if they had been subjected to some strange alchemy with the power to alter their substance, changing them into inorganic, artificial entities.

The interior of the villa was altogether different: the first time that I set foot inside it I was amazed to be confronted with a bizarre hybrid between dwelling place and workshop. The furnishings were plain and practical, the new walls made rational subdivisions of the space, but all of this was frustrated by a disorder which had reached the stage where it was extremely hard to determine the original function of each piece of furniture, while it was only the names assigned to the different rooms by the engineer which allowed me to recognise their purpose. I could not understand how a man who regarded the tiniest weed as a personal insult could put up with living in such a chaotic environment.

Perhaps this was why he preferred to receive me outdoors, sitting under one of the oaks with me, and only on wet days did he take me into his office, a ground floor room with a view at the back. Papers, covered in a layer of ash, were always scattered across his desk as if there had just been a violent gust of wind, books were piled up higgledy-piggledy on the furniture, leaving wide empty spaces on the shelves, and never once was I able to sit down in an armchair without first having to move some object which had no place there.

The impression of incongruity provoked by that room was heightened by the broad French windows which looked out onto one of the most beautiful spots in the garden, a large semi-circular flower-bed dominated by a neo-classical statue. It was a female nude whose slender immature form brought to mind Artemis, the most unreachable of Olympus's female inhabitants; she carried no quiver, but a marble greyhound lay beside her on the pedestal. I pictured the engineer sitting at his desk dashing off pages in hastily scribbled handwriting and at intervals lifting his eyes to the serene perfection of the white idol, and it struck me that this icy muse was very fitting for a poet of coldness such as he was.

Gradually I became aware that for Stiler the house was just a staging post, a kind of military encampment whose value resided solely in its strategic importance; perhaps he did not even see it, as he would not have been able to see his own eyes turning away towards the theatre of operations, while he devoted pathological attention to whatever was going on outside, even if it were the most insignificant of events.

Ever since I had been in the village he had not undertaken any of those short trips by which his stay the previous summer had been interrupted.

'It would seem,' I said to him on one occasion as we sat on the bench facing the artificial lake, 'your professional commitments have diminished somewhat.'

'Diminished? What makes you imagine that?'

'I have the impression that this year you are able to enjoy a very long holiday.'

'Holiday, my dear Bausa, is by no means an appropriate term. The thing is, you can see the outcome but not the labour which it requires, day in, day out. If I do not leave here, if I postpone my commitments, it is because I cannot abandon the garden.'

'You cannot?'

'Not for a single day. The consequences would be disastrous.'

'Though, if the gardener were to take responsibility . . .'

'The gardener must be overseen, like all the rest. Believe me. I have to stay, come what may.'

As he spoke he examined the surface of the lake, which the oblique rays of the sun enlivened with a wavering sparkle, and the lazy floating motion of the water lilies, and the grassy carpet on whose totally uniform green the shadows of the bushes were lengthening. This man, I thought, was now a prisoner of his property, through the same twisted law which binds two mortal enemies indissolubly together.

'It costs you a lot to keep the garden in order.'

'It costs me, I dare say, all my time and all my

energies; but you see, only at this price can any under-
taking be carried through successfully. Make an effort
to remember how the garden once appeared, for
example on the day when I had the pleasure of making
your acquaintance, and then look around, observe what
it has become.'

'I must tell you that it is now almost impossible
for me to superimpose the two images. They are so
different . . .'

'Exactly. As you see it now, this place is from start
to finish my creation; created almost from nothing, if
that does not strike you as a blasphemous way of
putting it, and moreover a never-ending work of
creation, without which everything would be reduced
to ruins.'

'Or it would return to what it was before.'

'That seems to me the same thing.'

'Nonetheless, it's my impression that you take your
duties as creator a little too seriously.'

'Because I know the power of chaos, of disorder.
Form, you too will discover before long, is an unnatural
state, which can be maintained by force alone: spontaneously, everything has a tendency to revert to
formlessness.'

'Then your project must be destined to fall.'

'Not at all. I am tenacious, Bausa, more tenacious
than any tree or bush can ever be.'

'More tenacious than nature itself?'

'Perhaps not, but I have intellect on my side. I am
able to foresee, to forewarn, to fall back on defences. I
have a thousand resources at my disposal to stem its
destructive will, and I do not hesitate to resort to them
whenever the need arises. I don't possess the sublime

resignation of those orientals of yours, with their readiness to worship nothing under the name of God.'

'Yet, engineer, you too exercise a destructive will. It seems to me at times that there is something dead in the garden, like a great negation. Yes, at bottom here too there is a kinship with nothingness.'

'If you amuse yourself by playing with words in this way ... Anyway, I do not doubt that if we pursued the argument you would end up getting the better of me. I am a practical man, a positive man, saving a flower-bed from weeds matters more to me than any philosophical dispute: I hope you will take this confession in good part and have some sympathy with my plain common sense.'

Ursula's theory, whereby the engineer was the devil personified, seemed confirmed by the clouds of smoke and sulphur in which I found him enveloped disinfecting the plants. He was spraying them with chemical-smelling substances and mercilessly amputating those parts already contaminated, to be burnt later in great purifying bonfires, and he endured my witnessing all this with ill-disguised annoyance, like a stage director forced to allow the presence of a spectator behind the scenes.

He would undoubtedly have preferred to show me the garden only in its perfect guise, without the laborious operations from which this derived being revealed to my profane gaze. Even the simulacrum of Artemis was sometimes violated by armies of ants which climbed up its white limbs with the uttermost lack of respect; to put an end to these aggressions, it was then a matter of locating the ant-hill and destroying it with a flood of boiling water. To vanquish snails and moths the engineer had recourse instead to cunning, with an arrangement of special lamps which attracted nocturnal insects or with insidiously inviting upturned bowls.

Of course there was no shortage of mouse traps either, these being rather more complicated, sometimes out-and-out masterpieces on which Stiler had applied his technical skills with particular cruelty. I could not but be disturbed whenever I thought of the way in which these little animals, while imagining that they followed an impulse of their own, would fall prisoner to some alien, ineluctable device, and, yielding to the speculative tendency which is typical of youth, I wondered whether freedom could ever be anything other than an ingenious trap prepared by necessity the better to ensnare us to its own purposes.

On the other hand the persecution of the birds had almost ceased, not indeed because Stiler had turned to milder counsels, but because his 'exemplary punishments' had achieved the desired effect: the birds now avoided the garden; on rare occasions one would see a flock flying over it and as it neared the property one would be struck by the sudden stilling of their song. That unnatural silence reinforced the impression that the garden was a universe unto itself, sharply separated from everything surrounding it, a universe governed by its own laws and pervaded by its own atmosphere, as if between that ordered strip of plain and the disarrayed throng of hills there were raised an invisible barrier. Everything in that silence assumed a greater relief: the hedges and the flower-beds, the little lake and the

gravel pathways, the statue of Artemis and the two
great oaks, stood out distinct and isolated, protected
from any mingling with foreign elements, and I often
had the impression not of seeing them in their reality,
but of contemplating them in a painting, in the closed
and soundless world that was bounded by the frame.

At the beginning of August I had to be away for some
time, since I had promised to visit a university friend
who was on holiday with his parents in a place not far
from there. A few days before, I told Stiler about my
departure, and he was saddened.

'Well, all I can do is wish you a good trip. If you
promised to go then you must obviously fulfil your
obligation.'

'I won't be gone for long, I'll be back in two weeks
at the latest.'

'All the same, we'll miss you. Admittedly, here the
days go by in a rush, a fortnight seems no time at all.'

'I can imagine. When you're so busy . . .'

'Yes, I have to acknowledge that the garden is enough
to keep me company, indeed, more than enough, I dare
say. If your visits have been such a pleasure for me, it
is certainly not because I have any fear of solitude. But
you see, Bausa, there are times when one does need to
talk to someone, to show someone else the result of
one's own labours so as to get a viewpoint, a validation,
and you, with your sensitivity, are the ideal person.'

'You flatter me too much.'

'Not so, not so, put aside your modesty: you should
take pride in your own virtues. Anyway, it doesn't
seem to me that I have paid you a great compliment,

nor said anything out of the ordinary. You are an artist, therefore it's clear that you are capable of judging the beauty of the garden better than anyone else.'

'Yes, an artist.' Doubtless those words had been uttered in all seriousness, and yet I thought I detected an irony by which I felt almost humiliated. 'If going around with a sketch pad under your arm makes you an artist . . .'

'I don't understand what you mean at all. In the first place, I haven't been aware of you going around with a sketch pad for quite a while now. At least, not in this neighbourhood.'

'The fact is,' I answered, slightly embarrassed, 'I'm going through a difficult period, taking stock of things.'

'Have you stopped drawing, by any chance?'

'No, I haven't stopped.'

'So you use your sketch pad, you don't just carry it around under your arm: you, dear Bausa, *create*, you create images and forms, you create, in your own manner, order out of disorder, and as a result . . .'

'I have a feeling, engineer, that this term fits you better than me.'

'Fits me? I am a practical man, I think I've already told you so. I'm a mere technician.'

I smiled. 'Put your modesty aside, you should take pride in your own virtues.'

'Then be good enough to explain to me why the description of artist would fit me rather than you. It's true, you still have a long way to go; as I have had occasion to explain to you, you still lack that self-control . . .'

'You're mistaken, engineer, that is not the reason.

59

What you like to describe as romanticism is in fact a form of detachment, and therefore of self-control.'

'However, if I may say so, a self-control rooted in a lack of concrete participation, in an incapacity to act. A weakness, rather than a strong point. Of course I am talking in quite general terms.'

'And I concur in quite personal terms. For this reason I do not regard myself as an artist.'

'Young man, you are sliding out of my grasp like an eel: you do not have any profession, you do not strike me as possessing the mettle of a scholar, and now you are also rejecting the label of artist. Tell me, then, how am I to regard you.'

'Perhaps . . . as a witness. Besides, is that not always how you have regarded me?'

He shot me a look of mistrust. 'Is that a reproach?'

'Not at all. You paint the picture, and I watch; what reason would I have to reproach you?'

'None, exactly, not even if things were really like that. When I too made use of you . . .'

'I have never thought anything of the kind.'

'And you're wrong. In one sense, I do in fact make use of you, as you do of me.'

'As I do?'

'Certainly, and there is absolutely nothing shocking about it. Reciprocal benefit, dear boy, it is the foundation of all relationships between men.'

'But in what way, may I ask, do I make use of you?'

'You say you are a witness: well, if you really insist, I'll grant you that. However if this is the case you have need of something to witness, without this something you would find yourself high and dry, so to speak. Yes, dear Bausa, don't take offence, but you too are one of the garden's parasites. An extremely welcome parasite, naturally.'

While I was a guest at my fellow student's villa, I thought back frequently to that conversation. The way in which Stiler had characterised me may have been blunt, it matched his habit of subdividing human beings into rigidly set types which eschewed their individual specificities with drastic simplification. I was in no doubt that the term 'parasite' in his eyes referred to a very precise category of which I was certainly not the only representative, a category diametrically opposed to the fertile and productive one to which he himself belonged. Yet I could not fail to recognise a funda-mental accuracy in his opinion, all the more so now that distance from the garden made me realise how I had focused my mind upon it a great deal latterly.

I never spoke of it to the friend whose guest I was, nor did I even speak about the engineer: often however, when I went for a walk in the big park, which was done in the English style, I amused myself by imagining the indignation that Stiler would have felt on seeing all those corners deliberately left in their wild state, the irregular arrangements of trees and bushes, the air of instability conferred on that place by the wicker easy chairs and loungers continually moved about, imper-vious to any dictates but the search for some temporary comfort.

I in no way shared his despotic ideal of natural beauty, on the contrary, observing the rigorous geometry according to which he had moulded the garden I had often found myself regretful for the metaphysical significance which I had once discerned in it, now erased by a will which was incapable of tolerating anything obscure: it seemed to me then that the engineer was unable to grasp in casual events the manifestation of an incomprehensible higher necessity, but considered them solely as insults, offences to his own sovereignty, like the little chicken bone which had so absurdly cut short his uncle's life.

And yet his vision of things managed to win me over, inducing me to compare any and every landscape with the ordered one of the garden. Thus my host's park, which precisely because the hand of man had intervened with a lighter touch, did indeed better match my taste, nonetheless contradicted another feeling, one rooted in me, in the weeks spent close to Stiler, with the imperceptible violence of habit.

This feeling, I realised, related as much to the garden as to its maker, without drawing any clear distinction between the two. A spiteful observer would perhaps have marked it down as the amazed envy of the parasite towards someone who has the means to create, or as the irresistible attraction which draws contemplative natures towards those impelled to action, as if to find in them the necessary complement. But what fascinated me even more was the fact – paradoxical only on the surface – that Stiler's restless temperament had been able to express itself in a work which was so balanced and harmonious, that all of his excesses had achieved translation into the serene classicism of those forms.

When my visit was finally over and I was able to return to the village, it was therefore the thought of the garden which inspired in me the relief of one returning to a homeland after a journey and ending a long-felt nostalgia. And as soon as I had reached the boarding house I opened wide the window of my room so that I could see, among the hills lapped by the last slanting rays of sunlight, the one at whose back the villa was hidden.

Looking down into the square, I saw a figure which I recognised as the engineer. Walking quickly and almost furtively, he went up to the post box, slipped an envelope into it and made off at once. Before he disappeared into an alleyway I tried to call out to him; he must have heard me, because he slowed down a little, but without turning round. A moment later, with a purposeful step, he had resumed his onward path.

The next day I went up to the villa, where I received a strange welcome. When I had taken my leave Stiler had been visibly dejected by that albeit brief separation. He saw no one else but me, he had chosen me as sole witness to his work, and for this reason I had imagined he would be impatient to see me again just as I was to return; instead he greeted me in an offhand way, as if we had parted the evening before, and at the same time with a detachment which made my absence appear much longer to me than it had been in reality.

'So,' I asked him when we had sat down under one of the oaks, 'have things gone well for you of late?'

'Very well, thank you,' he answered with an embarrassed smile which I had never seen before. It did not occur to him to ask me the same question. He sipped his cup of tea with unaccustomed slowness, as if sunk in deep thought; he seemed quite oblivious to the time he was wasting by idling, to the countless routine tasks which he was certainly neglecting.

He was so unamenable to any kind of conversation that I was very soon tempted to leave; but had I done so Stiler might have thought I was offended, and I did not wish to attribute excessive importance to what I then imagined was a passing malaise. So I had to stay on a little longer and meanwhile find something to say: and instinctively I said the one and only thing able to shake Stiler out of his apathy.

'Have you nothing new to show me?'

'New?'

'In the garden, I mean.'

He did not reply immediately. I realised that there was indeed something new in the garden, yet he hesitated to show it to me. For the first time since I'd known him he seemed uncertain whether to allow the presence of a spectator.

At last he made up his mind. 'Come with me,' he said placing a hand on my shoulder.

We headed towards the back of the house. From the pathway I discerned the statue of Artemis rising white on its pedestal. When we were close I saw that in the flower-bed in front of the statue red flowers formed a letter on the grass, a large Z.

'Z? What does it mean? It isn't one of your initials.'

'Z, my dear friend, is the last letter,' he replied quietly. 'The completion.' His eyes half closed, he was studying the marble creature with a singularly absorbed expression.

'I don't understand.'

'Of course you don't, Bausa. For you to understand, I should have to give you some explanations

which would be premature, and indelicate in relation
to . . . a third person.'

When a man talks about a 'person' in the reticent
tone with which Stiler had uttered this word, he usually
has a woman in mind. I therefore interpreted what he
had said as a veiled reference to some affair of the heart,
and yet it was hard for me to believe that he was in
love: in fact the engineer harboured a deep mistrust
of love, composed in equal parts of scepticism and fear,
regarding it alternatively as a sugary illusion to which
weak souls had recourse to justify their weaknesses,
and a destructive force, akin to the one against which
he battled with such fury in the garden. Perhaps
because he considered them as depositaries and instruments of such a force, he also withheld any liking for
women. In his view they were capricious, frivolous and
irrational creatures, who if not a danger to a tranquil
life were at the least a terrible nuisance, and woe betide
anyone foolish enough to invest his own hopes of happiness in one of them. Only in these altogether
unflattering terms, which were barely modified by
respect for propriety, had he so far referred to his own
female acquaintances, and I assumed these to have been
imposed by social obligations or else dictated by an
impulse of desire too lukewarm to outlast the initial
gratification. But that letter, that huge Z carved into the
grass, seemed to indicate a quite different sentiment.

We entered the office. The engineer was watching me
keenly, as if to detect my reactions.

'I should not want,' he said after some time, 'you to
have formed any mistaken idea.'

'I haven't formed any idea. I'm aware however that
something has changed.'

'No, I assure you, nothing has changed; it's merely a matter of logical, sequential development. And in a certain sense this comes into my project. You'll see, soon all will be quite clear to you.'

On the other side of the window panes, the marble goddess bent a cold, distant gaze on the flower-bed.

In the days that followed Stiler continued to present me with fresh evidence of his metamorphosis, exhibiting all the symptoms of love. If he heard the bell ring at the time when the postman usually came, he would brusquely cut short our conversation and rush to the gate himself, as if in fear that the maid would get there first. Once a week, with punctual regularity, he would go down to the village to post a letter. From the window of my room I would see him cross the square with that furtive manner which had so astonished me on the evening of my return, but I now made no attempt to call him; doubtless he would have pretended not to hear me.

One afternoon, as we sat in the office seeking some shelter from the noonday heat behind its thick walls, the telephone on the desk began to ring. The engineer gave me a look that was actually hostile, as if all at once my presence had become an intolerable hindrance to him. He wavered for a moment, perhaps weighing up the option of not answering, but the ringing continued; finally he made up his mind to unearth the apparatus from under the heap of papers which covered it and pick up the receiver.

'Hello? Yes, speaking,' he said, still staring at me with that not very friendly expression. 'Oh, what a pleasure. Well, thanks, and . . . how are things there? Right now I have someone visiting, so I can't talk for long on the telephone, alas. No, no, it's a pleasure, as I said; only, right now . . . Fine . . . No, I'll call you back as soon as I can. Of course, very soon. We'll speak later, then. Thanks, the same to . . . fine, we'll speak later.'

He put down the receiver. I had remarked that during this brief dialogue he had taken scrupulously childish care to avoid addressing the person by name on the telephone. He was obviously on familiar terms with this person, but it must have been a special kind of 'familiarity' in his eyes, one more intimate than that kept for friends and relatives, a 'familiarity' which reserve prevented him from expressing in front of me. That adolescent shyness both amused me and moved me, and when Stiler spoke to me again, his tone anxiously inquisitorial, I pretended to rouse myself from thoughts which had engaged me to the exclusion of listening to what had been said. This seemed to reassure him, and his manner very soon reassumed its customary cordiality; yet when I entered the office the next day, I saw that the telephone was no longer on the desk.

My curiosity to discover the identity of the person who had managed to provoke such sentiments in the engineer became stronger by the day. I had left him entrenched behind his perimeter wall, with the gardener's wife as his only female company, and to the best of my knowledge he had never left the place except to go down to the village.

Perhaps, I mused, the woman behind this was some

local beauty, or else someone on holiday. But my inquiries in this latter direction proved fruitless: questioned with circumspection, the boarding house landlady assured me that no young woman or girl had taken lodgings with her of late, and the small number of villas in the neighbourhood, old family possessions doomed to dereliction with changing fashions in tourism, had been closed up all the time. As for the local women, when I thought it over there was not even one of them whom I could imagine able to kindle so intense a flame in Stiler's heart.

I finally decided that I could only bring the enigma to light by putting aside all scruples and persuading Ursula to tell me what she knew. I therefore made my way up there, but instead of going to the villa I walked in the direction of the trim little white cottage that the engineer had built for his staff. It stood in a secluded spot, at the garden's edge, and it was largely concealed from anyone going along the main road by a hillock which left only a glimpse of the slate roof.

I had never gone near that house, nor could Stiler have been there recently, or he would have ordered the removal of the numerous features added by the tenants with the flagrant aim of neutralising the plainess of the architecture. Scattered on the carpet of grass were giant stone shells and plaster gnomes in bright colours, one raptly smoking a pipe, another leafing through a book, a third stretched out in an affected and indolent pose: the facade was completely covered in roses of every hue jumbled together without rhyme or reason, or rather with the intention of producing the most gaudy chromatic contrasts: this was an outright rebellion against the stark dictates of rationality, a naive nostalgia for beauty expressed in aberrant forms, provoking both condescension and respect alike.

No different was the aspect of the interior, where Ursula bade me enter with due ceremony. In the living-room, the few functional pieces of furniture bought by the engineer were submerged beneath an incalculable quantity of domestic paraphernalia conspicuous among which were an ashtray in the shape of a gondola, an enormous celluloid doll in Hungarian costume and a collection of gleaming copper pans hanging above the sideboard. On the shelves complete series of romantic novelettes were lined up, with titles promising stories of turbulent passion, each worthily capped with a proper 'happy ending'.

It took me a few minutes to get used to this over-crowded environment and to become aware that all the time I could hear a persistent medley of sounds, the most prevalent being a kind of composite twittering. I gave the lady of the house a questioning look.

For a moment, she appeared doubtful. Then she spoke, 'Yes, I feel that I can trust you. Come with me.'

She led me to the end of the corridor, into a little room opposite the bedroom, to which she gave the sophisticated appellation 'my personal *boudoir*'. Covering the walls were rows of cages in a great variety of shapes and sizes, and locked in the cages were doves and sparrows, mice and squirrels, every kind of animal to be found in the countryside, two by two, as in Noah's Ark.

'They are safe here. But I must ask you, sir, not to say anything to the engineer.'

'Don't worry: my lips are sealed.'

I sat down in one corner, on a stiff little upholstered

armchair. Even though the living-room sofa was doubt-less more comfortable, I thought it worth enduring some discomfort so as to avoid the oppressive company of the doll.

'You are a good person, sir, I always said so,' Ursula pronounced as she sat down opposite me. 'If only everyone were like you . . . But unfortunately there are heartless people in this world.'

'And yet, of late one might be tempted to think that even those people have a heart.'

At these words my interlocutor thoroughly bright-ened up. She smiled at me with an air of superiority, like an initiate face to face with a neophyte, and said nothing in answer.

'Or perhaps I'm mistaken?' I pressed.

'Is there something I can get you, sir? I've just made some lemonade.'

I accepted, and she left the room. I was not concerned by her reticence, I understood that as a seasoned story-teller, she was merely delaying in order to quicken my interest. And indeed, when she came back, as the glasses full of lemonade stood neglected on a side table, with extraordinary compliance she allowed me to extract from her a full account of what had happened.

So I learned that one afternoon, during my absence, an automobile had arrived and stopped outside the gate of the villa. The local people had not seen many auto-mobiles; and this one, according to Ursula, was an extremely luxurious model, huge and gleaming, its beauty such that it left her resigned to lamenting how poorly words could do it justice. It was raining, and everyone was indoors, but the roar of the engine made them run to the window. Or rather, the servants ran, while the engineer unhurriedly came out of his office, seeming, if anything, to be irritated by this unexpected event.

The only person to get out of the vehicle was a young lady, and what is more from the driver's side, so that one was compelled to yield to the evidence and acknowledge that it was she herself, something almost unbelievable in those days, who had driven the car there. From what could be seen, the young motorist was a thorough amalgam of womanly elegance. No one in those parts had ever set eyes on such a dress: it seemed to move by itself, as if it had a life of its own, and moreover it must have been quite waterproof, as was the young lady's hair, for while she stood waiting in the rain both hair and dress remained miraculously undampened.

The engineer advanced towards her with an umbrella and after a brief exchange of words held out his hand. From that distance and with the windows closed, Ursula could not have heard the laughter with which she answered him, but she unhesitatingly described it as 'silvery'. Then, instead of shaking his hand, the young lady threw her arms round his neck and kissed him on both cheeks. From this gesture, to which, also because of the umbrella, the engineer responded with much awkwardness, Ursula deduced that 'this charming creature' was a relative of his or else a childhood friend.

The two of them spent the whole afternoon together in a room which neither I nor the servant could refer to as 'the drawing-room' without a smile, where the occasional armchair floated in a sea of books and magazines piled up on the floor in eternal expectation of being tidied away. From the other side of the closed door could be heard a buzz of conversation of which the zealous narrator had not managed to make out a single syllable, and besides, of course, nor had she attempted to, but nonetheless she was able to state without fear of contradiction that the engineer addressed his guest in a tone of voice never heard before. Instead of talking, she maintained, it was more as if he cooed, just like one of those doves up there in their pagoda-shaped cage, and the young lady's speech certainly sounded no less affectionate.

Ursula was not qualified to say exactly what they had been cooing about all that time; the young lady did not ask for anything to drink, the engineer as ever demonstrated a distressing temperance, and so the door remained inexorably shut until the moment of farewell, when there emerged from the drawing-room a cloud of smoke, the charming creature and the master of the house, in that order.

This circumstance, together with the dim illumination in the entrance hall, where moreover the couple had scarcely lingered, as well as the unfortunate failure of the lights on the driveway perhaps occasioned by the rain, ensured that the profusion of adjectives, laudatory and vague in equal measure, with which Ursula endowed the person of the 'young lady', gave no precise matching description of her appearance. She was very beautiful, indisputably so, the entire edifice of conjecture which Ursula built up being founded upon this axiom; as yet, there was no way of knowing any more than this. Even that undampened hair, only partly hidden under a minute piece of headgear, lacked a definite colour, and the shade and cut of her clothes would alter obligingly, to suit every passing whim of imagination.

The stranger had finally left in the luxurious car, resplendent in the half light of that rainy day, carrying off her mystery and her freight of superlatives. And ever since then, Ursula concluded, with a tender glance at the pairs of animals in the cages, the engineer had not been the same.

As was to be expected, Ursula did not regard me as the only one worthy of hearing her confidences: it was not long before the engineer's romantic secret was divulged to the entire village and very soon it became a habitual topic of conversation at the café tables. There were remarks of all kinds, but every one of them essentially came down to one single, very simple formulation: 'How are the mighty fallen.' This man who was so different from everyone else and so proud of his own difference was now the victim of the commonest of passions, and because of this he became suddenly exiled from the higher sphere, beyond the vagaries of chance, where he had presumed to place himself with so much arrogance.

Now they would see who was stronger, that little man who was a bundle of nerves with his pathetic despotic ways, or the force before which they had always bowed in resignation, with no claim to inquire upon its meaning or its nature. In the case in point, this nebulous force was embodied in the equally nebulous person of the 'young lady', who was invested with the power to return or reject Stiler's love, and the people of the village, in overwhelming majority, made no secret of their preference for the latter outcome.

All the same, perfumed envelopes continued to reach the Post Office with the engineer's address written on them in an elegantly slanting hand, and their contents grew ever more voluminous; if to start with these were merely notes, now the postman, feeling their weight, had to acknowledge that they were proper letters, three or four pages long, and when studied through the envelope these sheets appeared closely written, with hardly any margins. His letters on the other hand remained invariably one page long, and what is more the paragraph breaks were very frequent. Against the light you could see compact lines surrounded by big white spaces, so that the engineer would have been suspected of sending poetry to his lady love, had not his reputation as a practical man rendered any such supposition unlikely.

However the case might be, they continued to write to one another assiduously, and with their epistolary exchanges becoming even more intense with the passage of time. Within less than a month of my return there began to be rumours among the country people that the villa would soon have a mistress.

I do not know what formed the basis of this prediction: Stiler did not talk about his private affairs even with me, except by vague reference, and Ursula, whom I had initially regarded as the most likely source of this gossiping, refused either to deny or confirm it, presumably dressing up what was effectively her ignorance about the engineer's plans in the noble disguise of reserve.

For my part, I had trouble believing that Stiler would

ever decide to get married. It would have been too grave an incongruity, a flagrant contradiction of his whole way of being and of thinking. And yet I was often reminded of the words which he had uttered that day, at the feet of the statue, in front of the flower-bed in which red flowers traced the mysterious initial: 'Z, my dear friend, is the last letter, the completion.'

This new passion did not distract him at all from the garden. Stiler continued to devote all his energies to it, as though he had no other aim in the world, and I did not understand how he could split himself between two objects, each one of which should have made full claims upon him. But in the end, I reflected, it was not that strange after all: his behaviour put me in mind of how a bird might work with alacrity to build a nest, or rather, to keep it in perfect order while waiting for a mate.

One day, as we were sitting together beside the large flower-bed, I purposefully turned the conversation towards the subject of marriage. 'It is fortunate that you are a bachelor and without children. Fortunate, I mean, for the garden. Running wild with their games as they do, children often cause more damage than mice or birds.'

His look, until that moment lost in contemplation of Artemis, turned towards me from the statue with sudden severity, and I saw that the provocation had touched its mark. 'In the first place, Bausa, there are children and children; a lot depends on the way in which they are brought up, and someone who was able to inculcate a sense of discipline in his own children early on would have no reason to fear damage.'

'Though it can't always be done . . .'

'In the second place,' he went on, strangling that attempted interruption at birth, 'what else is the child but the man to come, he whose turn it will be some day to continue our work and preserve it from destruction? The man who gave up procreation for the sake of his work of creation, only to discover too late that he had no one to whom he could entrust it, would truly choose the fool's way.'

'And yet, an heir can disappoint expectations.'

'Only when there has been a failure to educate him with one's own goals in mind. For a son, and this is the third point which, if you will allow me, I want to add to those I have already made, is in another sense a work of creation, and in another sense the incarnation of our will, the product and crowning achievement of our labours. From this it follows that marriage . . .'

'An institution to which I imagined you to be firmly opposed.'

'Not at all, I am not opposed in principle.'

'In principle?'

'Unless I'm mistaken, young man, we are in fact talking about principles, and with no reference to personal choices. Regarding the latter, my intentions, assuming that I have any, will be made known to you in due course.'

For the first time the coherence of his reasoning did not strike me as a spontaneous talent, but as the result of an effort masking some inner conflict which remained unresolved. The sun was by now far from its zenith, and the shadow of Artemis lengthened on the flower-bed, intersecting the great Z.

'Of course,' I said, almost thinking aloud, 'from the point of view of the garden . . .'

'What, I beg your pardon? From which point of view?'

'I was thinking that the image, or if you prefer the symbol of the garden, seems to require a female presence for its own completion.'

'Yes, I think I see what you mean. Your theory, I must acknowledge, is very interesting; for some time now I've been coming round to the idea that the garden and woman, if we keep our argument in abstract terms . . .'

'For example, an Eden without Eve would be quite unimaginable.'

He gave me a puzzled stare. 'Eve? My dear Bausa, you could not have chosen a more unfortunate example. Luckily your idea is of greater value than the arguments you adopt to sustain it. An Eden without Eve . . . And I suppose you judge an Eden without a serpent to be equally unimaginable. Yes, from this line of reasoning you'll end up asserting that the symbol of the garden requires a diabolical presence for its completion.'

'It's a fascinating suggestion.'

'Oh, without a doubt; it goes hand in hand with your theology of a God who is also nothing. But how would you feel about leaving aside the sacred Scriptures and considering the garden in a more profane light? After all, we are not talking about a metaphysical place, but simply . . . a place inhabited by man. If we want to be precise, about a space which man wrests from nature in order to mould it according to the laws of his own intellect.'

'If you like, I am willing to accept this definition. But within this kind of perspective I'm unable to see what role our Eve can fulfil.'

'I'll explain to you at once, Bausa. You will acknowledge that in a purely logical respect, man and woman
are complementary terms.'

There was something touching in that recourse to
logic. 'Not just in that respect, as far as I can see.'

'I am keeping to what concerns the subject of our
discussion. We are not talking about feelings, that is
not the point.'

I could not stop myself from smiling. 'In a purely
logical respect, engineer, feeling is the bond which con-
nects the two complementary terms, whereby it does
not seem to me altogether alien to our subject.'

'You are displaying an unaccustomed inclination to
sophistry today. And then, if you'll allow me, I can't
see what you are driving at: you keep on contradicting
me, and yet the view you hold is no different from
mine. Or perhaps it is your intention to deny that
woman . . .'

'I'm not denying anything.'

'In that case, must I infer that I have your approval?'

'My approval? I should never have imagined that it
mattered so much to you.'

'I am obviously referring to approval of my argument. Unless I'm mistaken, you are my interlocutor,
therefore it is natural that I should set myself the aim
of persuading you to agree with me.'

'You want to persuade me to agree about something
on which anybody would concur.'

'All the better, dear Bausa. What interests me is to
be right, not to furnish evidence of originality.'

'Well then, you are right: you have my formal state-
ment of it.'

'Thank you. It's not that I doubted it, it's always a pleasure however to see one's own opinions shared.'

And ending this peculiar dispute without adversaries, he resumed looking at the statue, his face gradually taking on a calmer expression.

I often wondered what name the big letter outlined in the flower-bed stood for. I knew very few women's names beginning with a Z, and moreover they were all somewhat unlikely: I could not be persuaded that the elegant young lady who had arrived in the car was called Zita, or Zaira, or Zobeida, or worse still Zenobia; perhaps the initial indicated some pet name, but I was incapable of establishing which. For this reason in my thoughts I always referred to the unknown woman as 'Zee', and I wound up almost convincing myself that this really was her name.

Little by little I too was conquered by the charms exercised by that woman who continued to dominate Stiler's mind from the realms of absence. However, the malady, transmitted by such indirect routes, struck me in a slight, benign form: it consisted mainly in my absurd and yet unvarying attempt to reconstruct Zee's appearance on the basis of the scant details at my disposal.

Usually she was just a small figure in floating garments, standing next to a huge car; at other times I amused myself by guessing at her features in a kind of incorporeal portrait; from their vagueness and constant alterations, these assumed a protean character which with the passage of time I ceased to ascribe to the incompleteness of my information, but saw as emanating from her, as if her true being resided precisely in that hypothetical nature, in that elusive multiplicity.

My uncertainty had by now shifted onto its object to the extent that I was convinced all of these women who were so different, either blonde or dark, with features that were aristocratically angular or else soft and unpronounced, like a doll's, were so many images of Zee, each of them with an equal right to claim fidelity to its model. And I was increasingly beguiled not by Zee, but by the perennial fluctuation of forms whose source she was.

Nor perhaps did Zee's authentic personality carry great weight in the engineer's project, which was beginning to become clear to me even though he never spoke of it explicitly. Her visit must have upset him like an intrusion of disorder into the inviolate geometry of the garden, until, in this particular woman who had turned up out of the blue, he saw *woman*, the generic and necessary complement, the last letter of an alphabet which he fondly imagined he could master.

As the days went by I became aware that Stiler and I were not the only ones to cast our thoughts towards the mysterious visitor; the fact was that after a while Ursula began to complain to me about the bad influence the young lady had upon the engineer. This influence, as I myself was able daily to observe, took the form of a fresh interest in the house, in an attempt to stem the anarchy which until then had reigned there. Whereas before, her master's indifference had allowed Ursula virtually to neglect her own duties, so that all she did was make the bed, serve a meal thrown together twice a day and do a bit of summary dusting whose value was primarily symbolic, now every least failing was immediately remarked upon and taken up as the pretext for a rebuke which gradually extended its reach to include the entire running of domestic arrangements.

'A slave on a chain, sir, that's what I've become. And it'll be even worse after the wedding.'

I however had my doubts that plans had yet been made for this marriage which, ever since the day of the visit, Ursula had regarded as something altogether bound to happen. His long isolation had made Stiler more vulnerable; outside impressions, being such a rarity, acted upon him with extraordinary intensity, so while it did not surprise me that a few hours spent in the company of a woman had been enough to make him fall for her, the possibility that she would agree to marry him struck me as rather remote. A refined and beautiful city girl, whose life doubtless abounded in meetings and distractions, would not easily let herself be persuaded to take as a husband a man of such lacklustre habits, and Stiler must have been aware of this; yet he pursued his 'project' with calculated patience, writing to her every week, making a furtive trip down to the village to post the letters. He pursued it with serenity, as if he were sure of its success, so unshakeable was his faith in his own power to tame fate and bend it to his will.

Although after secondary school he had given up the study of philosophy, deeming it a vain imposture unworthy of an adult mind, he very much liked to quote the words of a Greek thinker who had made a deep impression on him, that famous fragment according to which character is man's destiny. Now, given the circumstances to which he usually applied this maxim, it became clear that for him 'character' in no way signified the ensemble of an individual's moral and psychological lineaments, but was more a synonym for 'backbone', for resolve. A man of character is master of the random, is not someone who dies from swallowing a little chicken bone; a man of character always gets the woman he has chosen, so long as the choice is the outcome of a careful calculation and not a pointless whim. Because therefore he trusted in this perfect matching of his character and his destiny and maintained the desire which prompted him as the most rational one there could be, I do not believe that he gave any serious consideration to the possibility of a refusal on Zee's part. He seemed to face the most important events in his life with the same confidence with which he asked for small favours.

I imagined his love letters composed in the same style as the two or three notes which he had sent to me, a meagre, pared-down style, almost bereft of adjectives. Reading what he wrote, it was rare to come across a subjunctive or a conditional, moods and tenses which I favoured because of their oblique nature, because of what could be described as the reserve which holds them back from directly grasping their own object. Perhaps it was this very reason which impelled him to avoid them as much as possible and to prefer the imperative or the indicative, above all the future indicative. The thoughts expressed by him were in fact almost always instructions, unequivocal directions which moved firmly from the present towards the future, while the necessarily inert memory of past time took up very little room. Thus, when he addressed Zee, he would certainly not dwell on recalling their first meeting, but would in the event propose other meetings, and describe them in every detail.

This speculation was reinforced by the presence on his desk, which was now kept in perfect order, of a railway timetable always open at the same page. One day I finally asked Stiler if he was planning to go away.

'Yes, I have it in mind. If the garden were to allow me some breathing space . . .'

'Is it to be a long trip?'

'Just a few days in town, to pay someone a visit. I've been entertaining this idea for some time, but as you can see I keep putting it off.'

He cast an irritated look at the white Artemis. Despite his new passion, he was still a prisoner of the garden, but it now seemed that this oppressed him. For a man like him to want to do something and have to give it up was without a doubt the worst of tortures, and he endured it in a state of rancorous resignation.

'And yet,' I said, 'I have the impression that everything is going wonderfully here.'

'That is my impression too, but it is not reason enough to lower one's guard. No, I really cannot leave right now.'

Autumn came, forming ever wider stains of red and yellow among the green of the hills, and gradually it began to slide into winter without any alteration in the engineer's manner of living. He did not get around to putting the railway timetable back in its place, nor to leaving the garden; he nurtured plans to go way and refused to admit even the possibility of their being carried out. Meanwhile the correspondence continued, followed with growing curiosity by the people of the village, who still waited for some development to occur and who, with every day that passed, were increasingly disappointed in their own legitimate expectations.

I felt some regret at the idea that I would soon be back in the city, abandoning Stiler to solitude, but my company did not succeed in alleviating the deep dissatisfaction which seemed to have him in its grip, and the spectacle of sumptuous decadence which nature presented in that season doubtless did not help to improve his humour. On the few sunny days we walked together among evergreen shrubs and others whose leaves, having undergone their autumnal change of colour, were already beginning to fall, and when we walked beside the semi-circular flower-bed from which the big Z had disappeared some time earlier, my friend paused to look at the statue of Artemis. There was something painful in witnessing this now ill-endured confinement, so different from the self-imposed isolation of the year before, so it was with relief that I watched the date of my departure approach, when for a while I would be able to avert my eyes, and perhaps also my thoughts, from the now melancholy figure of Erasmo Stiler.

One afternoon, during a stroll, we were both afflicted by a chill such as we had been unused to feel for months and which now caught us quite by surprise, as if it were an unnatural condition never experienced before. When we got back, the engineer ordered Ursula to light a fire in the drawing-room hearth. We sat there for a long time as the room gradually heated up, often stretching our hands towards the flames. Outside, the garden was plunged in a premature twilight, which was also faintly disconcerting for the summer creatures we had become.

'Tell me, Bausa, how do you usually spend Christmas?' Stiler asked all of a sudden, his musings clearly inspired by this presage of winter.

'Christmas? Usually with my family, or rather, with what's left of it.'

'Oh yes, that's what I imagined. And if you had no relatives left, I suppose you would invent some for the purpose,' he remarked, giving me a look in which the irony was mixed with a strange sweetness. 'You are a sentimentalist, my dear friend, I shall never tire of saying so.'

'Like everyone, engineer, no more nor less. At Christmas even the most solitary individuals seek out the family, or for want of anything better, as you say, they invent one for themselves.'

'I, to give you an example, have never done anything of the kind. Ever since I lost my parents I have always spent Christmas alone, keeping busy with my usual occupations, and that's how I shall spend it this year. I have never allowed a mere date written in red on the calendar to undermine my habits.'

'Really? Not even when you were a child?'

'Children, Bausa, are precisely that: children; it's natural for them to let themselves be enthralled by these superstitions.'

'So you too let yourself be enthralled.'

'I too, certainly, but only up until the age of ten. I remember for example . . .'

He stopped short, and became engrossed in staring at the flames.

'For example, engineer?'

'Nonsense, nothing that merits being mentioned. Besides, you too must still carry the images of some day like that in your memory, with the glittering tree, and the presents wrapped in coloured paper, and the whole family gathered together, aunts and uncles, and cousins . . . In those days even my great-grandfather was still alive, an extremely old man but still lucid, enduring the prospect of death with extraordinary serenity. Of course I am aware of this now, thinking back on it; then, it could be said that I was ignorant of the very thought of death, as perhaps all children are ignorant of it.'

'Yes, I think it is so. At that age, death is something which does not concern us.'

'Which means, you see, nor could I understand how astonishing was the continuity of life. The concrete continuity, that is, the kind that is passed on from father to son. This is nonsense too, I know: real continuity, the only sort which distinguishes us from animals, is something different, it is handed down from one generation to the next thanks to what is created by the spirit, the intelligence. And yet it was really astonishing to see how my great-grandfather's features, and even some of his expressions or unconscious gestures, reappeared in his children, and in his grandchildren, and in his great-grandchildren, mixed up with others, having undergone variations, yet still recognisable. Yes, my friend, sometimes it seems to me that it is really a pity to leave the world like this.'

'Like what?'

'Like me.'

'You are still young, you cannot know for sure . . .'

'Maybe not. In fact, latterly I have often found

myself thinking . . . After all, Bausa, nothing is impossible, you only need to understand what you want in
time.'

'And you have understood?'

He smiled, and moved towards the hearth to rekindle
the fire.

'The Christmas tree . . . It's stupid – don't you think?
– to feel nostalgic for such things.'

On the eve of my departure I went up to the villa to say
goodbye and went through the gate without ringing, as
was my custom. When I got to just a few steps from
the house I heard the engineer's voice issuing from a
partly open window.

'I am compelled to contradict you, dearest.'

I stopped in hesitation, thinking that someone was
with him, but I very quickly realised that this was
instead a telephone conversation. Discretion forbade me
from entering, curiosity did not allow me to walk away,
so I stayed where I was, motionless, listening.

'I would be stubborn, as you claim, if I were wrong,'
Stiler was saying, 'but given that I'm right . . .'

A very long pause followed, and I was amazed that
Stiler was listening for so long without once interrupting.

'Excuse me, why do you maintain that you understand me when you don't understand me at all? . . . Of
course, otherwise you would not insist upon asking me
for something which is impossible . . . It's true, you
didn't insist, but you make me uncomfortable with
these roundabout ways of yours, I would by far prefer
a frank, direct response. You say I'm right so that you

can go on serenely thinking that I'm wrong... Yes, don't deny it, you are convinced that I'm wrong, that this is just a whim...'

He spoke in the peremptory way with which he was accustomed to uphold his own opinions with me too, without in the least softening his argumentative harshness; to all appearances, love had had no effect on certain aspects of his personality, and this discovery comforted me, I don't know why.

'You say I'm obstinate? It's possible, no, in fact, of course I acknowledge it. What's more: I regard it as a compliment.'

I smiled, thinking that he would soon launch into a eulogy of the straight line like the one he had taken up during one of our first discussions. Instead he calmed down all of a sudden and continued the conversation in a tone which Ursula would have described as 'cooing'.

'How can you say such a thing? You surely don't seriously believe that I don't want to see you again! Only, right now... No, naturally it won't always be like this, it could be that in a few weeks' time... All right, we'll talk about it again... Yes, of course, I do too...'

He lowered his voice, so that I was no longer able to hear it. I imagined that he was saying goodbye to his interlocutor and I hurried away; if he had surprised me there, he would have immediately realised that he had been spied on. I had almost reached the gate when Stiler called out to me.

'Bausa! Where are you running off to?'

I turned and saw him coming towards me. 'I thought you weren't at home,' I said, confused.

'When have you ever chanced to find me not at

home, at this hour? I hope I didn't keep you waiting for long.'

'Don't worry, I've just got here.'

So much the better. Come, let's sit down under the oak; it's a nice day today, it's good to be outside.'

We took our seats at the little marble table. If we looked up, we could see bright patches of sky edged by the dark mesh of branches.

'So, Bausa, you're leaving tomorrow.'

'Yes, alas.'

'Excuse me, why "alas"? This city is magnificent at this time of year. In fact, let me say, it may be that later on I shall decide to follow your example.'

'Really?'

'For a short spell, that's understood, when up here nature will be asleep under the snow and won't be in a condition to do any harm. Why not, dear Bausa? What would be wrong with that?'

'Absolutely nothing, engineer.'

'Exactly, absolutely nothing. Clearly, it would be quite a different matter if I were to go away now: that would amount to an unforgivable desertion.'

'It seems to me that you are exaggerating.'

'I'm not exaggerating at all, and I am amazed that you too . . . I am amazed that you do not realise what my duty is.'

'Towards the garden?'

'Towards myself, my dear friend. Above all towards myself.'

'Perhaps your first duty towards yourself is not to give up what you wish for.'

'Please, don't talk rubbish. Satisfying one's own

desires is certainly pleasurable, but to consider it actually a duty . . .'

'And yet that is exactly what it is: all of us are entrusted with the task of developing our own individuality in the most complete and harmonious way possible, and how can we hope to succeed in this if we make ourselves sacrifice certain things, if we do not allow every feature of our character, every aspect of our lives to unfold freely?'

'You really are very young. If you want some advice, forget all these fine theories, at least when you're painting. Your complete and harmonious individuality, with no choices and no sacrifices, would be expressed only in works that are begun and left unfinished. I have taken the decision to finish something, in so far as it is in my power.'

'I fear that such a decision is doomed to bring unhappiness to the man who is bent upon it.'

He shrugged. 'In that case, every human creature would be unhappy. Does not the very fact that we are men mean correcting nature, repressing some instincts in order to follow others?'

'If that were so, engineer, humanity would be nothing but a particularly ferocious form of discipline, an endless series of amputations.'

'And all of that frightens you, doesn't it? Sometimes it frightens me too, but I would find it much harder to endure . . . the absence of a goal. Yes, that would really make me afraid, that defenceless self-abandonment to nothingness.'

'Yet, as some people say, nothingness is one of God's names.'

He gave a faint shudder. 'But as others say, dear Bausa, we must cultivate our own garden.'

At my city apartment, where the alternations of the seasons can be apprehended almost solely from the hours of daylight, I often imagined the flower-beds covered in snow, the trees bare and livid, and my friend Stiler spending his days in the rigid solitude which he had imposed upon himself. In the beginning I expected that he would really come and spend the winter in town, but after some time, having received neither letters nor telephone calls from him, I came to view it as increasingly unlikely that I would see him away from the garden. Stiler, I concluded, had not carried out that 'desertion', not even to join the woman with whom he was in love; he would stay and watch over his creation, without any interruption, protecting it from the assaults of disintegrating forces. His illusion of being able to do otherwise was merely further testimony to his infatuation with Zee.

In the days around Christmas, every time I saw a decorated tree I would recall the nostalgia which he had expressed that afternoon, almost in spite of himself, and I guessed how the absence of that family warmth with which the celebrations had been gladdened when he was a child must have caused him much more pain than he would ever admit, more pain than there had ever been before the passion for Zee took control of him. Rising up so suddenly and violently, it had stirred the stagnant depths of his inner life, bringing to the surface images long forgotten, desires long dormant, but for the sake of what he regarded as his duty towards himself, Stiler opposed all of this with implacable resistance.

That renunciation, that solitude moved me, and I was impatient to return to assuage at least a little with my presence the dejection in which I pictured the engineer immersed through the long winter months, yet it was already almost summer when one morning I boarded the train which deposited me in the little village station after the two-hour journey.

Even before unpacking I made my way to the villa. I turned the last bend in the road, and parked next to the gate I saw a car with highly polished bodywork. As I looked at it I was joined by Ursula.

'Is this the young lady's car?' I asked her after a cordial exchange of greetings.

'No, sir: it's the engineer's car.'

'The engineer's? And since when does he own an automobile?'

'He bought it in town, this winter. I thought you would already have seen it.'

'The engineer has been in town?'

'He stayed there for a couple of months. Good heavens, sir, don't tell me that you never met him!'

'I thought he had spent the whole winter here. He didn't even get in touch with me on the phone.'

'Really? Hmm, in one sense it's more than understandable, sir, and you have no reason to be offended. You see,' she continued, lowering her voice, even though there was not a living soul to be seen in the whole hollow, 'it's not hard to guess why he went to town, and who he saw there. In love, you know, two's company.'

'Oh yes, that's it, as you say. I suppose that now the

engineer comes and goes very frequently, with the new automobile.'

'No, no, not in the least; since the end of winter everything has gone back to the way it was before, just the same. He hasn't left here once, he has too much to do, he says, and the car's only use is to give more work to that poor husband of mine, who has to polish it all the time, or else it'll rust. For people like us, sir, every change is a change for the worse.'

Ursula's lamentations brusquely came to a halt, and as I followed the direction of her eyes I observed that Stiler was coming down the gravel pathway towards us at a rapid pace.

'Dear boy, you finally made up your mind to come back! You're well, aren't you? You're looking extremely good. But I see you've noticed my automobile.'

'I was just admiring it.'

'Ursula is bound to have told you . . . I spent some time in town, Bausa, but there was really no way . . . You'll forgive me.'

'There's nothing I need to forgive, engineer,' I replied with a certain coldness.

'So much the better, then. You know, I took advantage of the brief truce the garden granted me. Now, unfortunately, we are in the thick of battle again.' He stopped short and turned a surly glance towards the servant. 'I'm sure, Ursula, that you'll find something to do in the house, I should like to entertain Mr Bausa on my own, if you don't mind.'

'Yes, sir, I'm going,' she mumbled, and set off towards the villa.

'Well then, engineer,' I said when she had left us,

'what's the news? Has there been some change since last autumn?'

'Has there been some change? It's strange, my friend, that you should ask me this question, because in fact in recent months some important events have come about.'

'Happy events, I hope.'

'Certainly, extremely happy, but unfortunately . . . not definitive. It takes time for events to reach maturity, and as I have already told you, the garden has allowed me very little time. If I think back over this winter, it all seems so remote, so unreal . . . It's as if I had taken a holiday from myself, and now the holiday is over.'

'Sooner or later you'll be able to allow yourself another one.'

'Yes, sooner or later. But come, I imagine that you will take pleasure in a stroll through the garden, after this long absence. I have replanted the red flowers under the statue of Artemis.'

Weeks went by during which the garden greeted the summer warmth with measured gratitude, I to'd and fro'd from the village, and the engineer was once more in the grip of a restless melancholy. It seemed as if he had never left that place, and I too was beginning to believe that the only purpose of the automobile was to burden Ursula's husband with another chore for his already wearied arms. Obviously the stay in town had not been enough to bring Stiler's love affair to a head nor to weaken his tie to the garden, so that it was again my lot to witness the bizarre spectacle of a hermit who ill endured his own cave but was incapable of leaving it.

This inner conflict became increasingly harsher, and Stiler's humour increasingly gloomy. On one occasion, while we were together in the office, Ursula came in to hand him a letter which the postman had just delivered, and when she had put it down on the desk I recognised one of the perfumed envelopes which had been so minutely described by the café's regulars.

Stiler, impatient, lifted it and slashed it open with the paper knife.

'You don't mind, do you? It could be news that I've been expecting for some time.'

He put on his glasses, unfolded the sheet of paper, and, as he read, gradually the excitement disappeared from his face, giving way to an expression of disappointment.

'I was mistaken, Bausa, there is no news. Would a little stroll suit you? I feel the need to stretch my legs.'

We went out through the French windows and walked past the big flower-bed without stopping, thereby taking the path which led to the little artificial lake. Stiler went over to the bank and set about scouring the gravel, picking up the largest of the pebbles.

'Do you need any help?'

'Help? I'm not doing anything, my friend, I'm only wasting time.' And he hurled the pebbles forcefully, one after the other, into this still water, which became immediately rippled with widening circles. He watched them disappear and remained a little while longer contemplating the lake, lost in thought; then, perhaps to justify his strange behaviour, he said: 'You see, today I don't feel well. Everything irritates me, and the garden especially.'

'The usual worries?'

'No, it's something quite different. It's a new sensation, which I myself can't really explain. Is it your view . . .'

'Yes? Go on, please.'

'Is it your view that one can live here?'

'It seems to me that you have been living here for a while.'

'That isn't what I meant.'

I understood what he meant, and it left me at a loss. 'Perhaps,' I ventured, 'there are aspects of life which are hard to reconcile with such rigour. The birds don't even dare to sing in your garden, which without a doubt does not help to make it a welcoming place.'

'I had certainly not aimed to make it a welcoming place,' he retorted drily.

'You asked for my opinion.'

'Yes, and I'm grateful for your frankness, but I should like to be understood better, at least by you. If in planning the garden I had let myself be guided by the criterion of comfort, of well-being, of personal happiness, it would be easy to accuse me of having miscalculated. Instead, I obeyed solely aesthetic laws. I tried to ensure that everything within it had a meaning, and I flatter myself that I succeeded: and this is the rigour which you are only too happy to criticise.'

'Beauty,' I objected, 'is not necessarily inhuman.'

'You think so? You know, when you talk like this I have the suspicion that you really are a dilettante.'

'I have never denied it.'

'You lack the temperament, my boy, the character. Perhaps some day you will realise that every outcome entails a degree of sacrifice: then you will throw away your sketch book, or else you will become cold, you will become an artist.'

'And I shall build places where it is not possible to live.'

He seemed troubled. 'And yet,' he said after a long silence, 'there must be a way of reconciling the two things.'

'Naturally: there are infinite compromises.'

'I am not searching for a compromise, I am searching for a solution.'

'Believe me, all this leaves me utterly amazed. I have always thought that you were satisfied with this place.'

'My dear friend, how could I not be? There is nothing that is not as I wanted it, nothing that I would change. At times, however, lately, I suddenly find myself looking at the garden with different eyes, I suddenly find myself almost . . . hating it.'

'It's a momentary depression, I'm certain; you'll soon get over it.'

'It wouldn't take a great deal, I can assure you, but still too much, I'm afraid, to be within my power. Doesn't it seem ridiculous, Bausa?'

With an abrupt movement, as if to cut short these confidences, he turned his back on the lake, and after motioning me to follow him he set off towards the house.

The following week, on entering the café one morning, I found the regulars engaged in a lively debate. They were discussing, with every possible side of the question being aired, a matter whose precise nature was not immediately clear to me, but which concerned

Erasmo Stiler. Here is the proof, some were saying, that the business has reached its conclusion at last. But others differed in the most categorical manner: the unusual event was not really so unusual, for everyone knew that the engineer was not the sort to settle for what he had; on the contrary, he was always making fresh improvements to his property, and this was exactly why, it should be recognised, the latter had been transformed from the worthless thing it was into an accumulation of perfections. The first group shook their heads in the face of so reductive an interpretation: had not the van driver, in person, when questioned in that very café, stated that along with the other furniture he was transporting an extremely luxurious dressing table? And was this not an unmistakable clue? Quite unconvinced, the other side objected that the driver had not said a word about double beds, and that where there is no bed there is no wedding, but the adversaries shrugged their shoulders with a scornful air at this retort; people of standing, they said, are peculiar: sometimes even when they are married they sleep in different beds, and even in different rooms. Frequently a member of one or other faction shot me an inquiring look in the hope of finding their propositions confirmed: I however went on pretending to be absorbed in reading the newspaper.

After paying my bill I hurried to the villa. As I arrived I saw the van parked outside the gate, with labourers busy unloading the latest furnishings under Stiler's watchful eye.

'Come in, come in, dear Bausa: just a few more minutes, and I'll be completely at your disposal.'

'What's going on? Did you decide to refurbish the house?'

'Exactly. Or rather, I decided to give this house a more welcoming appearance.'

He showed no trace of the sadness with which he had been overcome latterly; on the contrary, his whole demeanour intimated a joyous excitement. I tried to keep up with him as he followed a porter carrying a very large lampshade. 'It must have been a spur of the moment decision, you've never talked to me about it.'

'Fine, take it upstairs, the maid will tell you where to put it. And I urge you to be careful.'

When the porter had disappeared through the main door, Stiler addressed himself to me once more. 'You see, sometimes talking is just a waste of time: if one means to do something, it's better to get on with it without delay rather than discussing it with other people. And then, in a certain sense it really was a spur of the moment decision. A few days ago I learned that I'll soon have guests . . .'

'You don't say?'

'Your astonishment, Bausa, is in no way flattering. After all, I'm a sociable man, it's natural that from time to time I should receive visits.'

'Why not? More than natural.'

'Don't misunderstand me, I don't deem your company to be inadequate, quite the contrary, I value it very much. Nonetheless . . .'

'I understand very well, engineer.'

He eyed me with severity. 'I doubt that you can understand: your declaration strikes me as rash. At any rate a lady will be coming, an aunt of mine, accompanied by her daughter. I shall be pleased to introduce you to them.'

'And I shall be pleased to make their acquaintance. When will they arrive?'

'In roughly a week. There was no way of persuading them to settle on a precise date, they are so . . . disorganised . . . Like all women, moreover; there is a deeply rooted tendency to approximation in the female temperament. Apart from that, they are excellent people. I saw them often this winter, when I was in town, and last summer the daughter was here too.'

'I understand.'

'The reason why you keep on saying "I understand", dear Bausa, escapes me altogether. Returning to my cousin, she happens to be a rather attractive young woman, as you will be able to see for yourself. I'm very keen to have you meet her.'

That afternoon, as I returned to the village, the nature of the confused emotion aroused in me by the announcement of Zee's visit was already beginning to be apparent, and within a few hours it was clearly identifiable as apprehension. I was tempted to leave before she arrived so as to avoid that encounter, or at least to postpone it; I even remembered the forthcoming wedding of a distant relative of mine who lived in town, and all at once I felt myself obliged to be present at the ceremony, although on receiving the invitation I had had no scruples about throwing it in the waste basket and merely sending a telegram I dashed off.

This need to avoid Zee could seem inexplicable, even contradictory, after all of my fantasising about her. In fact, curiosity has always been one of my liveliest instincts, but even then, moulded and tempered by its first disappointments, it had become transmuted into a disinterested thing, a game which was an end in itself. The impulse had not weakened, yet, instead of seeking out some satisfaction which would have compelled it to transfer to a different object, I had learned to cultivate the inherent pleasure of its being suspended. I knew how dangerous it is to try and cross the ramparts of fire which protect the creatures of our fantasies, like sleeping Valkyries, from contact with reality, and this is why I held back from attempting anything of the kind.

If I make a comparison with Stiler's spontaneity, I have to recognise a certain lack of generosity in those timid wiles of mine: more rational than me, but perhaps less reasonable, he could never manage to make do with anything that was not the full and exact translation of idea into reality, and when I thought about the garden I could not deny that he had been able to give a tangible form to his own dreams without thereby devitalising them. His dynamism in the sphere of action was matched by an almost totally static consciousness, whose images seemed sculpted in marble like the white statue that watched over the garden.

And yet latterly a disturbing influence had crept into that mental landscape, cracking its stability, an influence which bore the name Zee. Only Zee and the burning desire to see her again could explain the strange rancour towards the garden exhibited by Stiler on the day he had received the letter.

Now I had the confirmation that when he had asked me if it was possible to live in that place what he really wanted to know was whether it was possible for two people to live there together, whether the joys, sorrows and inevitable approximations of a marital relationship could have a place there. Clearly, after his initial perplexities, Stiler had answered this question in the affirmative, yet I was convinced that what he aimed to achieve was a solution, not a compromise: he would never have contaminated the purity of the garden in order to satisfy his new requirements, but would rather have undertaken the difficult task of elevating everyday routines to that purity. In the picture which he was engaged in composing the figures would have to harmonise completely with the background, taking its distinct light into themselves.

When, a couple of days later, Stiler asked me to his house for dinner the following evening, I was astonished: in all the time we had known one another he had never extended an invitation of the kind to me, and, to the best of my knowledge, the table in the dining-room had never been laid. Usually he ate his meals in the office or else sitting at the little stone table under one of the two oaks, hurriedly, so as to expend as little time as possible away from his occupations; if I was present he would offer me a bite to eat with him, an offer which I, disinclined as I was to renounce the gluttonous pleasures which awaited me at the boarding house, would firmly turn down.

Now however it was not a matter of a simple snack, but of a proper dinner, duly announced and presumably organised with care, and all of this during a period when Stiler's contribution to our conversations was limited to an absent-minded greeting, a couple of laconic references to the weather or other topics of equal interest and a few words of farewell in which he curtly expressed his regrets for the countless burdens which prevented him from giving me his attention.

Zee, as I already knew, would shortly be arriving, and he had to devote all of his energies to the task of erasing from the house the traces of its long neglect. A squad of hourly-paid servants, headed with scant enthusiasm by Ursula, came and went through the wide open French windows, brandishing brooms, buckets and dusters; large bags filled with waste paper and old newspapers were piling up either side of the gate; it seemed that time and manpower were scarcely sufficient, though exploited intensively, to carry through the operations called for by the coming of the ladies, and now the engineer was deciding to sacrifice a portion of these for a dinner to which I alone had been invited. The inscrutability of that invitation made it impossible for me to refuse it, so on the evening agreed, at seven on the dot, I made my way to the villa.

Dark clouds, bluish grey in colour, had thickened in the sky; outlined like vast sailing boats, now and then they ran aground among the hills. In the garden the wind disturbed the geometric forms of the shrubs, restoring something of their lost natural state, and long invisible serpents seemed to coil through the grass.

The engineer was waiting for me in the office. I sat down in an armchair facing him, this time without needing to clear anything away so as to make room for myself. As we chatted about this and that I looked out of the window at the flower-bed in bloom, where the contours of the big Z gently swayed about, and at the marble goddess swathed in the livid light that preceded the storm as if by an emanation of her own, just as the moon dissolves the whiteness of her disc into a nimbus. Stiler too was looking at it, his expression now satisfied, now inexplicably worried.

Meanwhile my gaze had shifted to a perusal of the room. 'I don't see any new pieces. I thought you had changed the furniture.'

'All I've done is to make some additions here and there and I've prepared some rooms for my guests. Being women they have special requirements, it was my duty to provide for them.'

'The dressing table . . .'

'Precisely, and also more capacious wardrobes and other small improvements which I won't enumerate for you. But no frills of course: this is still my house, and consequently it has to respect my principles. Superfluous ornament, dear Bausa, is a crime against good taste, not just against good sense.'

'All the same,' I retorted, indicating the simulacrum of Artemis, 'that statue could also be described as superfluous.'

'Perhaps from the functional point of view, certainly not from the aesthetic. I am amazed that you don't grasp this.'

'From the aesthetic point of view, the boundary between the necessary and the superfluous seems to me extremely subjective. If you were to ask Ursula, for example, you would discover that on this matter she holds firm opinions that are radically different from your own.'

'You are greatly mistaken: that woman can have no firm opinions, simply because she is not equipped with solid and conscious criteria on the basis of which she could form any judgement.'

'Perhaps not conscious . . .'

'On the basis of my criteria,' he cut me short, 'that statue, in that spot, is actually indispensable, and the same goes for every detail of the garden. You said so yourself on one occasion: nothing here is left to chance. But you must forgive me, I am a very poor Amphitryon: here I am setting out my views on the beautiful, while the dinner gets cold. I had ordered it to be ready at eight, and it's already five past.'

Accompanied by the murmur of still distant thunder, like some discreet background music, we moved into the dining-room, a large room overlooking the access road, its only furniture an oval table surrounded by chairs of austere design.

I remember little of that evening's conversation, nor could I say what dishes were served; I recall only that these were considerably more elaborate than what I expected, and Ursula presented them with the attitude of someone being forced to pander to the whims of a spoiled child. Even her white apron and lace cap, which I had never seen before and which produced a grotesque effect on her bony figure, were paraded with a showiness which was by turns amused and exasperated, like some extravagant costume at a masked ball in which she was taking part against her will.

Gradually, the reason for the invitation became clear to me: this dinner was nothing other than a dress rehearsal with Zee's visit in mind. This was why Stiler, frowning, kept watch on Ursula's comportment, frequently correcting her with a curt word of command, while he checked the arrangement of cutlery and glasses and scrupulously inspected each course. He was about to sack the servant on the spot by the time three cigarette butts had accumulated in the ashtray without it having occurred to her to come and empty it, and when it came to carving the roast he created such a tense atmosphere that he made the knife shake in the poor woman's hands. As for myself, I felt like an intruder at that complex ceremony to which Stiler devoted all his attention, only now and then recalling that he had a guest at his table, albeit in the negligible role of guinea pig, and then saying a few words to me which I would answer with the certainty of not being listened to.

'A woman's presence is what's called for,' he said without warning, glowering in Ursula's direction as if to exclude her from this category, 'if a place is to be transformed into a real home.'

I made no comment, but I reflected that the place, the garden, had by now become for him the horizon which enclosed all future and all hope, to the point of impelling him to subordinate even the most intimate aspects of his life to it. Or perhaps this was only one way of justifying his own feelings to himself, by closing his eyes to their irrationality; losing his head because of a woman would have been a crime against good taste even more than against good sense, an inadmissible violation of the firm aesthetic and functional criteria which his actions had to obey; whereas making efforts to acquire the garden's indispensable complement in the form of a female presence meant fully respecting those very same criteria.

The thunder was coming closer, lightning streaked across the now dark sky with greater frequency. All at once we heard a crash, a rending sound, coming from nearby. We ran to the window: lightning had struck one of the oaks and a shifting foliage of flames danced around the great trunk. Rather than being doused by the downpour, it seemed to be invigorated, darting about furiously in response.

I stood there watching, mesmerised by the spectacle. When I turned towards Stiler I saw the expression on his face caught between rage and an ambiguous mixture of horror and repressed attraction.

For the first time I suspected that his will to domination, his stance of challenge towards nature which had so often led me to compare him to a Titan, in reality evinced a feeling for its sacred character. Where I went no further than contemplation, with the romantic detachment of the civilised man, Stiler faced the struggle against an adverse will, that of angel or demon, a heroic and blasphemous struggle, comprehensible only as the fruit of unavowed veneration. Perhaps not even he was aware of the magical, archaic background upon which he superimposed, palimpsest-like, his rational calculations, but some shade of this appeared in his eyes as he watched the flames be gradually extinguished to reveal the twisted nakedness of the stricken trunk.

'It's monstrous. Tomorrow without fail I shall have it cut down.'

He spoke these words in the tone of one who regards the matter as closed once and for all, yet he wavered for a moment before taking his eyes off the tree and moving away from the window.

✣ PART TWO ✣

WITHIN A FEW days, word had got round the village that two unknown ladies had arrived at the villa. The presence of the older one was unanimously regarded as irrelevant; as for the younger of the two, the locals remained in no doubt about her identity: the authoress of the perfumed letters, she who had been able to win the engineer's heart, was taking possession of what would now be hers by right. And those who had interpreted the delivery of the new furniture as the first intimation of a forthcoming wedding triumphed over the followers of the opposing party, who were reduced to mortified silence by this extraordinary event.

In the café, enthusiastic remarks were shed in equal measure upon the young woman and her automobile, the same adjectives being applied indiscriminately between the one and the other by turns.

The magnificent young lady had, as it happened, appeared in the village one morning, on board her magnificent vehicle, and had stopped right there, in the square, outside the café, to ask for directions. While her companion waited for her in the car, she had marched, bold as brass, through the maze of little tables and without the least hesitation or shyness had addressed the nearest group of regular customers. Such a free and easy demeanour was enough in itself to identify her as a city woman, a species for which the inhabitants of the village felt a certain suspicious admiration. What is more, such a creature could readily take the liberty of behaving in this way safe from any charges of indecorum: she had passed among the men gathered in the square as if she did not even see them, with the supreme insouciance which in their view marked the bearing of a 'true lady'.

This did not mean that there was anything haughty about her manners, on the contrary, the courtesy which she had shown when questioning the locals was in pleasing contrast with the brusque tone which the engineer used to talk to them. Because a 'true lady' is also kindly and polite with people of lower rank, which is to say she treats them as human beings and not as mere instruments for the satisfaction of her requirements; should she be in a hurry, a true lady does not let it be apparent, and in no circumstance does she allow her voice or her gestures to betray the slightest trace of irritability. Such angelic composure, they maintained, would be a veritable breath of fresh air for the owner of the villa; they maintained it with the overwrought satisfaction of someone who sees at last the advent of a yearned for vengeance, as if that 'breath of fresh air' were a punishment, a harsh lesson that the unknown woman had come to impart. They already pictured the engineer reduced to following this woman 'like a little dog on a leash', promptly obeying her mild commands, showing himself ever more docile, that is tamed and humiliated in his own titanic pride; and the state of mind in which they relished the prospect of this humiliation was anything but charitable.

Ever since the sumptuous automobile had driven off in the direction of the hills, they had had no further news either of Stiler or his guests; in those first days Ursula, undoubtedly busy seeing to the new arrivals, instead of coming down to the village would entrust the errands to her husband, an excellent man who however was not noted for his eloquence and seemed besides to have picked up from his master that hurried manner which inherently ruled out any possibility of conversation.

In such a sorry situation, it was natural that I should represent the only hope for them. Often, seeing me turn up at the café, they would ask if I was back from a walk or had one in mind, and when I answered in the negative they would appear simultaneously disappointed and incredulous: they simply could not understand why someone so fortunate as to be able to visit the villa whenever he wished should refuse to avail himself of the privilege at such a time, without realising that it was precisely the arrival of the two guests which stripped me of it, compelling me for the sake of discretion to await an explicit invitation from Stiler. And since the invitation did not come, the only thing I could do was combine my unsatisfied curiosity with that of the locals, listening to them as they endlessly repeated the story of Zee's brief visitation, each time embroidering upon it with variations and embellishments. In the course of that exile I drew a slim and elegant female silhouette holding a long rope in her hand. A male figure was tied to the other end of the rope and followed her walking on all fours.

At last one morning, as I was loafing about whiling away the time in the village square, I saw Stiler issue from a side street. He had come no further when he stopped and turned round, and a moment or so later two women appeared, one of them elderly, the other young, both wearing light-coloured dresses. Immediately, without my having any choice in the matter, all of my attention became focused on the latter, whose lovely slender figure I admired even from what I could discern of it at that distance. She advanced very slowly, and the hem of her skirt swayed about slightly in an echo of her movements.

So there she was, the object of Stiler's hints and reticent remarks, the elusive mystery woman whom I had attempted to approach with my conjectures; now I had her before me in flesh and blood, and the reality made its own claim, abruptly cutting short the tumult of speculations which for so long had stirred up my fantasies. This, and no other, was the figure of Zee, her hair was that exact colour, and the seal of concreteness in an instant made irrelevant all the constant fabrications upon which my imagination had been engaged until then. A mite daunted, I reflected that I would only need to go a few steps nearer to ascertain without any doubt the appearance of her eyes, her mouth, her features.

I still wavered, caught between warring impulses, when the little group shifted from its course and headed towards me.

'Dearest Bausa!' said Stiler with warmth. 'Do you remember my humble self, or have you forgotten me? This, my dears, is the friend I told you about, allow me to introduce him.' And he carried out this ritual impeccably, first pronouncing my name for the benefit of the ladies, and then the ladies' own names. Thus I learned that the young woman was called Zelda.

She must have been around thirty. Her face was perfectly oval, her delicate features had a classical regularity, her long grey-blue eyes gave me lazy, veiled looks, in which only momentarily did any glimmer of interest rise, and as I watched her I thought back on the mild and nonchalant young lady described by the people of the village in a portrait whose accuracy I could not have faulted. The fact that she drove the automobile, and perhaps even of her being related to Stiler had led to me to imagine her as energetic, strong-willed, almost masculine: instead in appearance and demeanour she revealed a femininity so marked as to border on frailty. Much of the time she kept her lips slightly parted, as if pressing them together were too much of an effort for her, or as if she were on the point of saying something but then, after thinking it over, decided it was not worth the trouble. In fact she spoke very little, mostly doing no more than listening to the meaningless phrases that her mother and I exchanged to moderate our sense of mutual strangeness, and when she took any part in the conversation she did so with a murmur whose unvarying softness of tone seemed somewhat more important than her words. Everything about her was attractive, her face and figure, her clothes and her way of moving and gesturing, but indolence was overlaid on these attractions like a film on the colours of a painting, attenuating in them a brilliance which would otherwise have appeared flagrant, and her charm was heightened by that seeming negation. Even the purity of her complexion allowed, as if neglectfully, the exception of the occasional tiny freckle which faintly dotted her cheekbones and the tip of her nose.

From the café tables the customers cast us surreptitious looks. I don't know what they were thinking at that moment about the beautiful incomer, or about her mother, a tall, thin woman in whom, despite her age, there remained a significant resemblance to the daughter, but in recompense I have no doubt about how they regarded Stiler's behaviour: if they had been able to express their opinion out loud, they would have said for sure that Stiler's eyes 'were devouring' the younger of his guests. He was so infatuated with her that he even tolerated the funny little name with which she addressed him: she called him 'Rasmi', an endearmeant which was certainly more suitable for a small dog on a leash than for a proud master of chance, and yet every time he heard it spoken Stiler seemed actually pleased. It was equally evident that his being thus designated in my presence made him more than a shade embarrassed.

We stood exchanging pleasantries at length beside the newspaper stand, without Stiler thinking to suggest we make ourselves more comfortable at one of the café tables. He seemed, on the contrary, anxious to conclude this pause, and consulted his watch with increasing frequency and obvious impatience.

'Well,' he would try to say every so often, 'it's been a real pleasure,' but his attempts at leavetaking foundered against the immobility of the two women, who lingered on more than anything out of inertia, and the engineer would console himself for his lack of success by lighting another cigarette. Blatantly the duties of hospitality were at odds with those he felt towards the garden, given that prolonging a conversation meant neglecting important tasks; yet he seemed to accept this enforced idleness with an unaccustomed compliancy.

At last the ladies decided to move on, after inviting me to accompany them for part of the way. Both mother and daughter proceeded slowly and we strove to adapt to their pace, something which was particularly difficult for the engineer. He would stop abruptly, whenever he became aware of having become too detached from the group, and I could not help but imagine that Zee had given a sharp little tug on the invisible rope with which she kept him bound.

We said goodbye at a fork in the road, just outside the village. Stiler urged me to drop in on him, and the two women gave me the kindest and most spontaneous assurances that a visit from me would also give them pleasure. I therefore promised to make my way to the villa soon.

'Please do remember,' said the mother, 'that we shall expect you.'

The daughter held out her hand. 'I too implore you,' she said smiling. She walked away, then turned to face me once more. 'Don't keep us waiting too long,' she added before setting off again with the others.

I stood there watching them for a little while as they climbed the path, Stiler always one step ahead of his guests and continually twisting round towards them with clumsy solicitude; then I headed in the opposite direction back towards the boarding house.

The very next day, in the afternoon, I went up to the villa. As a courtesy to the ladies I rang the bell, even though as always the gate was unlocked. As I waited I looked across through the bars and discovered that the oak struck by lightning had not been felled the day after the storm, as Stiler had manifestly intended. This bare and blackened tree made a glaring contrast with its verdant partner on the other side of the avenue, one which was doubtless intolerable in the engineer's eyes, but for me not without charm. The lightning had infused the oak with an arrested dynamism which I would have liked to reproduce on canvas: it seemed suspended in the moment before collapse, poised between survival and ruination, and the trunk arched itself touchingly, as if genuflecting before hostile divinities.

I was absorbed in this contemplation when Stiler joined me. He at once saw the direction of my gaze.

'Come, Bausa, let's go inside: that tree is anything but a pleasant sight.'

'I didn't expect to find it still there.'

'In fact you shouldn't have found it there,' he replied in an apologetic tone, 'but these last few days I have been very busy.'

'It's natural that it should have slipped your mind, with the arrival of your guests.'

'Slipped my mind? Not in the least. Don't do me the injustice of thinking such a thing. Let me tell you that on the very morning after that regretful accident I gave the gardener an instruction to ensure that the damaged oak was felled. As you can see for yourself, he has not done so.'

'Quite clearly.'

'You will point out that I should have reminded him about it, rebuked him for his sloth, and you are perfectly right: I shall do so, as soon as I have the time. The visit of my relatives makes me happier than I can express, but I have to entertain them, converse with them all the time even about the most trivial matters; and as if that weren't enough, that woman, I refer to my maid, is in no way capable of coping on her own, so that it's up to me to keep a very firm check on her. If you had seen the dishes that she had the audacity to serve to us last night . . .'

'Inedible?'

'I'm not talking about the substance, Bausa, but the form. Ursula is an excellent cook, yet in her manner of presenting food she displays such bad taste that I never cease to marvel at it. And then she is absent-minded, she always forgets something . . . You see, I require that my guests be served in impeccable style.'

'You're absolutely right. And the oak can always wait.'

He gave me a sceptical stare. 'Yes, it can wait. Tell me, though, what's your impression of my cousin Zelda?'

The directness of this question disconcerted me. 'What's my impression? I only spoke to her briefly.'

'You made up for it however, you won't deny, by taking a very good look at her. Is it indiscreet of me to ask you to convey the result of your observations?'

'The result, engineer, is more than flattering, and this certainly can't be any surprise to you. There is no doubt that your cousin has a beauty which is out of the ordinary.'

'A perfect beauty, my dear friend. It is only a pity about those freckles: she ought to avoid exposure to sunlight.'

'They are scarcely visible,' I said, suppressing a smile, 'and personally I find them delightful.'

'That's as may be. Nonetheless, you will have noted the regularity of her features, the proportions of her figure . . .'

He spoke about her in the same detached tone with which an expert would have listed the merits of a work of art, as if in his eyes Zee was no more than an ensemble of lines and forms combined in a particularly felicitous manner. Had I not seen him the day before almost intimidated by her presence, perhaps I would have let myself be taken in by this ostentatious objectivity.

'We had better go, Bausa: the ladies will soon be down in the drawing-room.'

We went up the avenue to the villa, and on the threshold Stiler turned for a moment before closing the door, and shot the lightning-struck oak a look charged with indignation.

Zee's mother (I could never manage to think of her as Zelda) had made a second marriage with an uncle of the engineer; not the chicken bone one, but another, who had died much more reasonably of heart disease. It was Stiler himself who told me all this while we waited for the ladies in the drawing-room. Ursula had bowed to his injunction and filled up the sugar bowl with extra lumps, though protesting that the few remaining from the morning were quite sufficient; then, without any end to her grumbling about the master's new notions, she had retreated to the kitchen.

The engineer sat down in his armchair in a pose that

was anything but relaxed, ready to leap to his feet the minute Zee and her mother should appear on the threshold, and when they finally arrived he greeted them in the most solicitous manner.

'Well done, you have kept your promise,' the young woman told me, then she turned her attention to the little table on which were laid the cups, the teapot and a large tray crammed with biscuits. 'If you don't mind, Rasmi, I'll see to the tea.'

'Why do you want to to put yourself out? The maid will take care of it.'

'Let her have her way,' the aunt interjected. 'She so much likes to play at being mistress of the house.'

These words altogether stifled Stiler's scruples; he sat down again, and in an attitude of devotion set to watching the slow, punctilious gestures made by Zee around the table. I too watched her, and quite suddenly, without being able to explain why I thought so, I got the feeling that for her movement was something unnatural, and that the indolence which had made an impression on me during our first encounter in the village was an instinctive precaution with which this perfect figure defended itself from anything undermining its perfection.

When each one of us was finally in possession of our own cups, the beautiful dispenser of tea moved away from the little table with a look of satisfaction and sat down on the sofa beside her mother.

The conversation, interrupted now and then by Zee's further manoeuvres around the teapot, touched on several episodes which had taken place during Stiler's visit to the city, episodes which were narrated and commented upon at length by the older of the guests, who took care to punctuate her prolix talk with repeated direct address to myself so as not to make me feel left out of these accounts, which on the contrary appeared to be delivered for my benefit. These were extremely banal happenings, yet there emerged from them an image of the engineer which was totally different from the one to which I was used: according to the aunt, it seemed that the moment Stiler had set foot in town he had changed from being a morose hermit into a sparklingly sociable man of the world and had acquired a singularly kind disposition, whose most manifest proof was the countless attentions with which he surrounded his cousin.

If my eyes alighted on Zee, such a change did not strike me as at all unlikely. One had only to look at the way she sat, with an absence of constraint that threw her spontaneous grace into even greater relief, to feel suddenly won over, and her manner of playing at being mistress of the house was so delicious that I could certainly not be surprised at Stiler's conceiving the project of turning game into reality. As for myself, I made do with thinking what a marvellous model she would have been for a portrait.

From the words which she now and then interjected to confirm or correct her mother's assertions, I very quickly realised that Zee held her cousin in the profound esteem due to superior minds, and simultaneously felt towards him that faint condescension usually aroused by eccentric types. The two states of mind however seemed to proceed in parallel, as if they referred to two different men: she had obviously never imagined that the slightest connection might exist between the engineer's eccentricity and his intellectual superiority.

Nonetheless, between the two there seemed to be a state of total harmony, and when I finally took leave of them and made my way alone towards the gate I felt incredibly euphoric; this meeting had entirely reassured me about the present and the future of my friend, I could go off with the comforting conviction of leaving him in a kind of paradise.

The visits that followed produced further features to back up my optimism. In this romance, it is true, Stiler acted his part like a clumsy beginner, yet no one watching him could have doubted the utter dedication with which he threw himself into his new role. Moreover, I believed I had never seen him so happy.

The house itself showed signs of sharing his happiness: it had been promoted from staging post to home, a much more rewarding function, and both Stiler and Zee strove to have it fulfilled as best they could, he maintaining the scrupulous order which he had established while awaiting his cousin's arrival, she mitigating this order with discreet little interventions. Thus she never came back from a walk without a small bunch of flowers exquisitely composed as decoration for the drawing-room or the dining-room table, a habit which at first had left Ursula completely at a loss: there had been no flower vases of any sort in that house, so that now a bit of resourcefulness was called for to unearth some contrivance that could be plausibly adapted to such a use. Carafes, teapots, ice buckets were therefore mobilised, without any regard for their more genuine vocation and legitimate expectations, and very soon the ground-floor rooms seethed with so many little green corners that they looked like a second garden, only more human and friendly than the one spread out around them.

By shifting things just a fraction, Zee had also modified the arrangement of the furniture in the drawing-room; whereas before sofas and armchairs were rigidly aligned against the walls, as if to display a mutual indifference, now they turned towards one another to create an impression of open sociability. Stiler did not just tolerate these innovations, he seemed actually to delight in them. He readily spent more time in the house, and when we gathered around the little table in the drawing-room he exhibited no great haste to interrupt the conversation and busy himself again with his chores.

They often alluded to childhood memories, Zee freely expressing nostalgia, the engineer concealing it with a veneer of irony, and once, thanks to allusions of this kind, I discovered that in those Christmas reunions which Stiler had recalled in a moment of abandon the previous autumn, besides the glittering tree and the presents wrapped in bright coloured paper, besides the aunts and uncles and the long-lived great-grand-father, the presence of his charming little cousin had an importance which was by no means negligible, if not for the child of that time at least for the man of now.

It had in fact been Stiler who, on one of those occasions, with a few curt words had dispelled from the little girl's mind any belief in the existence of Father Christmas, disclosing to her the rather more prosaic source of the gifts which she would find beneath the tree. Perhaps it was exactly then, with the tears provoked by her brusque disillusionment scarcely dry, that

Zee had begun to form the high opinion of her cousin for the sake of which she now showed herself inclined to return his feelings.

The meeting of the two former childhood companions after years of separation, their distant kinship, with no bond of blood as its basis, the way in which love had cunningly caught unawares a man who would have put up strenuous resistance to a less sudden seduction, all contributed to endow Stiler's matrimonial plans with the blessing of the ineluctable. If ever life kept a bride in waiting for such a solitary individual, this bride, I was sure, could only be Zee. Her character seemed moulded on purpose to make a salutary contrast with that of her cousin, compensating for its shortcomings, balancing its virtues and faults with opposite virtues and faults.

If my thoughts returned to that far-off afternoon, when the automobile had stopped outside the gate of the villa for the first time, and to how the two had met, imagining this through the romantic transfiguration in which Ursula had presented it, it no longer seemed so strange to me that a single conversation should have been enough to introduce so powerfully into Stiler's mind the idea of having found in Zee the woman who was made for him: after all, I had reached the very same conclusion almost as quickly.

Some time passed before I began to fear that I had formulated a rash judgement. From what I remember, it was during one of our by now habitual gatherings around the tea table that I first noticed a faint crack in the pre-established harmony to which I had trustingly attributed the capacity to govern relations between the two cousins down to the smallest detail. We were returning from a walk in the garden which had fuelled Zee's mother with a voluble enthusiasm.

'It is so lovely here,' was her verdict, pronounced as she fell back exhausted on the sofa, 'that I regret not having come sooner.'

'Yet, aunt, it was certainly not a pleasant place at the start. Our friend Bausa can tell you about the state of dereliction in which I found the property.'

'And it has to be said,' I announced at once so as to extricate myself from this task, 'that the engineer has worked miracles.'

'Yes. Rasmi's uncle was really wonderfully inspired when he named him his heir,' said Zee. She let out a little sigh, then added: 'Poor thing, what a dreadful end! Whoever would have predicted it?'

'No one, my girl, absolutely no one. But alas that is our lot: here today, drinking tea and chatting away happily and tomorrow . . .'

'It was a dreadful quirk of fate.'

These words spoken by his cousin had the power to wrench Stiler out of the torpid beautitude into which he had plunged. 'Fate? If you'll allow me, dear Zelda, it does not seem the appropriate term. Why ever do you want to ennoble the blind ferocity of chance in this way?'

'Don't get angry, Rasmi,' she said in astonishment.

'I'm not getting at all angry; I merely do not concur with your lexical choice; on the contrary, I refute it in the most categorical manner. "Fate" sounds too lofty a word for . . . for that little chicken bone.'

Zee seemed to greet his criticism with total indifference.

'I haven't exercised any lexical choice, all I did was use the first expression that came into my mind.'

'Bad, Zelda, very bad. Often approximation . . .'

'Then you tell me how you want me to define that accident. Nothing changes the facts, though, whatever word you use to describe it.'

'Not the facts, you're right, but our attitude towards them changes. You see, talking about a dreadful quirk of fate already implies submission, surrender.'

'If you prefer, I'll say it was a dreadful stroke of luck. Mummy, can I pour you some tea?'

'Dear Zelda,' insisted the engineer, who seemed to have the ground cut from under his feet by his interlocutrix's compliancy, 'I wish you would make an effort to understand . . .'

'Of course, dear, I understand very well. Now, please, settle down and let me serve tea.'

This dialogue was very instructive for me. It taught me the only way to make sure one got the better of Stiler in an argument: to refuse to be drawn into it. Perhaps it was instinct that had prompted Zee to resort to this method, one as infallible as it was elementary, and yet I did not believe it was a matter of a mere expedient adopted for this instance. Even then, and increasingly as I got to know her better, I discerned in Zee's very indolence something fleeting, something elusive, which was all of a piece with the lazy slowness of her gestures.

It must have been precisely this apparent meekness which attracted the engineer, persuading him that he was dealing with a very pliant material which he could mould according to his own intentions, a terrain from which he could uproot anything he deemed to be out of place as he uprooted the weeds from the well-tended flower-beds in the garden. This being so, my friend was the victim of an error, since meekness of this kind in no way signified a defect of character: Zee was stubborn about not wanting in the same way in which Stiler was stubborn about wanting; lack of willpower constituted her fundamental and unalterable attitude to life. And I wondered whether any real bond would ever be possible between two people one of whom was perennially intent on pursuit and the other on evasion, or whether Zee might not always slip through the fingers of whoever tried to catch her.

In one sense, it was clear, she was extremely willing to be caught, her flirtatious style of 'playing at being mistress of the house' plainly spelled out that the engineer's intentions would find a favourable reception. But a Zee tamed, reduced like the garden to conformity in everything and for everything to Stiler's will, was something I could not really imagine.

The more I saw of her, the more I glimpsed a secret and tenacious strength in her docility. If, to induce an interlocutor to accept his opinion or satisfy his wish, Stiler had recourse to rational arguments or attempted to bend him with a display of energetic determination, Zee just as unfailingly achieved the same end, but she never chose such direct means: with the unwavering stillness of a spider waiting for its prey at the centre of the web, she would be patient until that opinion or that wish were so much imbued with the charm with which she expressed them that they in turn became seductive, almost irresistible. Nothing was more pleasant than submitting to her will in this way, and I myself delighted extraordinarily in every little courtesy that I had the chance to perform for her, without realising that it was in fact Zee, with her subtle and thoroughly tactful skill, who continually offered, indeed imposed on me, such opportunities.

As for Stiler, his demeanour towards his cousin was a bizarre mixture of paternal severity and enamoured submissiveness. In words, he adopted the intransigence of a pedagogue to scold this woman with whom he had played as a boy; in action, he did everything in his power to please her. Thus the pathological fear of even the most inoffensive insects exhibited by Zee often prompted long remonstrances by Stiler, indignant about this display of irrationality, but it did not stop him from having thick-meshed mosquito screens placed on the windows of the room where she slept.

'You see, Bausa,' he said to me once, as if to explain himself, 'with women what is needed is firmness in the strategy, but a certain indulgence in the tactics. They have to be soothed and corrected simultaneously, just like children.'

I did not reply, yet it seemed to me that Zee, while allowing herself to be soothed with flagrant gratification, was refractory to any attempt at correction. Despite the engineer's efforts to make her stay agreeable, she was loath even to make herself at home and continued to go around the garden as if in an alien world. She professed admiration for this or that detail, declared herself happy to be 'in touch with nature', but I felt that she did not succeed in really loving that life. Sometimes, as we sat outside on those late summer afternoons, her eyes would rove around the circular barrier of the hills, the sheer blue of the sky, and the ordered garden where no birds sang. 'What peace,' she would murmur, and a shadow would darken her pale irises.

One day, for teatime, Stiler had a small table brought out to the back of the house along with some garden chairs, perhaps preferring, rather than the view of the lightning-struck oak, that of Artemis, who, from her solitary position at the back of the flower-bed, seemed to turn her face haughtily away from us. Absorbed in her own thoughts, Zee was drumming her tea spoon against her cup and taking no notice of the tender looks cast towards her by her cousin.

'It's a pity there is no piano here,' she said suddenly in a melancholy tone. 'At home I play every day.'

'Her playing is heavenly, Mr Bausa,' her mother hastened to announce. 'Like an angel in Paradise.'

'Come now, Mummy, don't let's exaggerate: I've got no personal experience whatsoever, but I imagine that the angels are much better than me. It's nothing more than a hobby, an old habit, which I'm very fond of, however.'

'Of course you're extremely good,' replied Stiler, 'and it's always a pleasure to listen to you. But speaking in general terms, I cannot share this excessive passion of yours for music.'

'It appears you haven't changed in the least,' his aunt told him, laughing. 'As a boy, whenever you came to visit us, you couldn't stand hearing Zelda play: being such an *enfant terrible*, you had downright tantrums to make her stop.'

'No, I haven't changed, at least from that point of

view. I mistrust music as I mistrust alcohol and everything which clouds consciousness.'

Zee stretched her spine against the back of the easy chair. 'Yet it's so nice to let oneself be clouded, now and then . . .'

'Aunt, I advise you to keep a close watch on your daughter: she could turn into an opium smoker. A thinking being must always remain its own master.'

'Ah, without a doubt, you are absolutely right. Only, I fear that's the way for your thinking being to end up bored to death,' Zee remarked.

'I am never bored.'

'If you'll allow me, engineer,' I interjected, 'I think your position is based on an error, or rather, on the disavowal of a fundamental truth.'

'Well then, Bausa, it's up to you to enlighten me. What might this fundamental truth be?'

'Simply, that music does not belong to the category of stupefying substances, but to that of the arts.'

'It seems to me that Mr Bausa is not entirely wrong, Rasmi,' Zee cautiously approved. 'Perhaps, if you compared it for example to painting instead of alcohol . . .'

'Painting,' retorted Stiler, 'is an art of clarity, music an art of obscurity. I do not see how that intolerable stirring up of formless emotions can be compared with the seeking of form.'

'Yet painting too has to do with emotions. Or am I mistaken, Mr Bausa?'

Stiler did not give me the time to reply. 'In those cases, dear Zelda, the fault is entirely the painter's, and his incapacity to understand the true essence of his art. However, what is visible is always limpid to some degree, and sound too, whenever it expresses a meaning.

But if instead of acting as an instrument of thought, sound lays claim to being an end in itself, then it becomes a turbid, irrational element.'

'I don't want to contradict you,' said Zee, in whom the habitual reluctance to argue had obviously been overwhelmed by an impulse to defend the art she so loved, 'but perhaps this element you described as irrational is not a prerogative of music; perhaps it is a part of our nature.'

'My dear, by good fortune we are not just nature: with will, with intellect, we are able to raise ourselves above the confusion of our instincts.'

'That's very true,' exclaimed the aunt, her face lighting up. 'For example, we have learned table manners.'

'A great advance, without doubt, though from what I can see musicians hardly eat with their hands.'

'They do worse than that, Zelda: they compose.'

'However, no one will succeed in convincing me that things are as you believe. After all there isn't just reason, and a sorry thing it would be if there were, and often life too develops a tortuous progress, just like some melodies.'

'My dear, man is neither an octopus nor a crayfish: leave your tortuousness to those inferior species.'

Zee shook her head resignedly: 'Mr Bausa, would you say something too. We crayfish have to give one another some mutual support, after all.'

We went on arguing for a long time, but we could not induce the engineer to modify his own opinions by a fraction. Yet that same evening, as he accompanied me to the gate, Stiler asked me if there was any way of renting a piano in the area. I replied that I would make inquiries and he urged me not to mention it to his cousin: so as not to spoil the surprise for her, he declared, but perhaps his real reason was a desire to hide that immediate surrender.

From then on, Zee established a jocular complicity with me at the engineer's expense, an alliance of youth against the rigour of maturity. She would often call on my help to get the better of any argument, would talk to me at length about music, and involved me in playing checkers or other games in which Stiler had always refused to take part, declaring that she preferred me as a partner rather than 'that grumpy Rasmi'. She had also taken to calling me by my christian name. But on my side the familiarity diminished whenever Stiler was absent: alone with her, I felt confused, awkward, and all of a sudden I would seem to have nothing to say to her. Perhaps that embarrassment was the natural reaction of a young, shy man face to face with a woman to whom he was unconsciously attracted, or perhaps even then I had plunged into the role of observer to the point where I was unable to assume any other, in the same way that I could not have appeared in a picture I was painting.

Thus, adopting quite knowingly for the first time a stance which I would always maintain throughout my life, I reflected on the relationship between Stiler and Zee, pondered the state of mind of one or the other, but was always careful to keep myself out of the picture; above all, a certain instinctive prudence prompted me never to think about Zee except with reference to the engineer and never to ask myself whether I liked her. I wish I could make it plain that this decision was dictated by a sense of loyalty towards my friend, but I doubt that this was the true reason. What was demonstrated in that period, and which made the company of Stiler's beautiful cousin almost painful for me, was rather a deep repugnance for any active participation in life, a vertigo which compelled me to stay well away from the edge in case I should fall. Yet my 'parasite' nature drew a valuable nutriment from the development of the bond between Zee and Stiler, and registered it avidly, making it the object of complex intellectual alchemies.

With increasing frequency, as I watched them I became aware that I was witnessing not so much the romance of two people in love, as a struggle in which sides had to be taken for one or other of the adversaries. A bizarre struggle, since to all appearances both of them were aiming for the same objective. The engineer wanted to marry Zee and Zee, for whatever reason, wanted to marry the engineer: absolute harmony prevailed between them on this point. It was merely a matter of settling which of them would hold the leash, and in this respect I could not help but harbour the keenest anxiety for Stiler's future. The fate of the garden, no less than that of its creator, depended on the outcome of the contest, and whenever I happened to pass by the large flower-bed I had the impression that Artemis was giving me a worried look. Even the greyhound's face had lost all its snootiness, expressing only a downcast reproach.

One evening, as the fiery colours of sunset were already burning in the sky, I found Zee sitting on a bench close by the flower-bed. She was alone, contemplating her initial which stood out purple against the green of the grass. Suddenly, seeing them so near one another, I observed a singular resemblance between the divinity on the pedestal and the engineer's cousin: the regular features, the oval shape of the face, everything, except the freckles, made them alike; they seemed a pair of twins, one of whom had chosen as her manner of living that marble existence removed from alteration, while the little marks on the face of the other were the flagrant sign of a compromise with more changeable spheres.

As soon as she noticed me, she invited me to join her. My presence seemed to offer her some inexplicable relief.

'Come here, Daniele, sit down next to me. I was admiring my flower-bed; it's really magnificent in this light. It was such a lovely thought of Rasmi's, so nice ...'

'I'm glad you appreciate it,' I said taking a seat beside her. 'I too have a particular fondness for this corner of the garden.'

'I was really just referring to the flower-bed. I have to confess that the rest isn't quite to my taste.'

'Why is that?'

'I couldn't say, it's only a vague impression. Look, for example ... the statue. Don't you find there is something hostile about it, something threatening?'

'Threatening for whom?'

'For no one, of course, we are talking about a piece of marble. And yet when I sit here I feel ill at ease, as if I were an unwelcome guest. But this is idiotic, please forgive me.'

'On the contrary, all this is very interesting.

However, if you feel ill at ease you could avoid this part of the garden.'

She smiled. 'I certainly won't let a statue stop me from admiring my flower-bed. Though you must admit that she looks unfriendly; not to mention the dog, I'm amazed it hasn't bitten anybody yet.'

'Poor beast.'

'Yes, do take its part ... But I beg you, don't say anything to Rasmi: he would be upset, and he really doesn't deserve that. It was such a nice thought of his ...'

'Don't worry, you can count on my discretion. Besides, I doubt that the engineer is willing to listen to the slightest criticism of the garden.'

'My cousin is very stubborn, and lately, from what I see, he has saved up all his stubborness for this place. He doesn't seem able to part from it for even half a day.'

'Yes,' I answered, recalling the nervousness shown by Stiler when we had paused to make conversation in the village square, 'it's a well-ingrained habit by now, almost a vice, I'd say. Just think that in the village they've nicknamed him "the hermit".'

'The hermit ...' She was not looking at me, and continued to stare at the hills, whose green, in the dying light, had altered little by little to a deep black, like velvet. 'You know, Daniele, I think this garden's failing is that it has no view. The hills close it in on every side, and as a result one feels oneself ... in prison.'

'Which is why you don't like it?'

'I've never said I don't like it, but there is no doubt that it has an extremely bad influence on my cousin. Compared with last winter, when we saw one another in town, he seems quite a different person. That was when he was really himself.'

'Are you sure it's not the opposite?'

'The opposite? Come now, Rasmi has always been sociable, with lots of interests . . . Whereas now it looks as though for him the world has shrunk to this piece of ground.'

'Actually, there is some truth in what you say.'

'Never mind, it's an infatuation which has to run its course, like an illness. Sooner or later he'll get better.'

I said nothing. Zee got up, and together we set out for the house, leaving Artemis to enjoy her own solitude.

That evening, on my way back to the village, my thoughts returned to the disquiet shown by Zee. It was certainly strange that her aversion towards the garden had focused on her marble twin, though such an aversion perhaps hid an unconscious jealousy in which a female figure, albeit inanimate, was the most natural object.

Obviously she had not noticed her own resemblance to the statue; I however had noticed it, and I could therefore imagine Stiler's amazement when he found himself face to face with his cousin. As I had been told, the two of them had not seen one another for fifteen years, during which time Stiler had completely neglected his relatives in order to pursue his profession; glimpsing Zee beside the automobile, he must have believed for a moment that Artemis had descended from her pedestal, and that ideal of beauty had been mysteriously made flesh in a mortal woman. Perceiving the latter as his predestined bride, the future mistress of the garden, meant drawing an obvious conclusion, and although by now the engineer realised that his cousin was not just the living copy of Artemis, but a creature possessing quite autonomous thoughts and opinions, which were often in contrast with his own, the force of that primitive identification remained untouched for him.

Moreover, that side of Zee's personality which contradicted every principle of marmoreal composure, and which in my own mind I summed up as the freckle side, intensified Stiler's feelings rather than attenuating them, tingeing them with tender indulgence. Perhaps, almost in spite of himself, he was beginning to discern the charm of imperfection, even little chicken bones taking on a more tolerable aspect in his eyes when they appeared not as the revolt of an inimical nature, but as the caprice of that young woman who was so attractive and affectionate.

The walks, which for Zee were always disappointingly short, seemed to me instead an irrefutable demonstration of Stiler's new compliance, of his wish to please his cousin. He regarded it as necessary for the well-being of his guests to give them now and then the opportunity to 'get about a bit', but if they had explained to him that the principal reason for their outings was the wish to change their surroundings, he would undoubtedly not have understood, being convinced, and rightly enough, that it was impossible to find any landscape in the area that could bear comparison with the garden.

In every case he always scrupulously fulfilled what he considered to be his own duty, even though he never strayed far from the house, and almost always invited me to join the small party. Sometimes we stopped for a light meal in one of the small local restaurants, or else we would choose some secluded spot to spread out a makeshift table on the grass and eat the filled rolls prepared by Ursula.

Often during these walks it was up to me to entertain Stiler's aunt, while he walked beside Zee, or to be more precise in front of her, since he had not yet learned to adapt to her slow pace.

The old lady kept the conversation going almost single-handed, and since she was irremediably set against any discussion in general terms she would always end up telling me anecdotes that had some relation or other to the childhood of Zee and of Stiler. The two cousins, between whom there was an age difference of exactly ten years, saw one another fairly seldom: usually, in addition to the Christmas festivities, on 'official' occasions like christenings, weddings or funerals. As early as the age of four, Zee displayed, as her mother put it, a distinct *penchant* for the future engineer, though he was at that time a secondary school student and as such did not even deign to look at the little girl, or rather, would not have deigned to look at her had his relatives not been in the habit of giving him the annoying responsibility of keeping an eye on her during those family gatherings.

Once, at a marriage ceremony, Zee was particularly *charmante*, dressed in a white frock which had sparked the enthusiasm of all the aunts; she wore a wreath of flowers on her head and her hair, at that time blonde and only faintly flecked with copper, was tied into two long pony-tails at the sides. After lunch the little girl wanted to go out and play in the park, and young Rasmi was obliged to accompany her. Not a jot impressed with her *charme*, he began leafing through a book which he had providentially brought with him, while she, jumping around him, did everything she could to disturb his reading. All of this was subsequently learned from Rasmi himself, who, however, according to my zealous informant, always tended to portray Zee as much harder to put up with than she really was.

In exasperation, the boy then closed his book and transferred his attention to his cousin, when he suddenly noticed that one of her pony-tails was slightly longer than the other. He was so irritated by this that he made up his mind to remedy it straightaway; he ran into the kitchen and got the cook to give him a pair of scissors, giving evasive answers to her requests for explanations, then he went back into the garden where the unknowing and trustful Zee awaited him; he gripped the longer of the pony-tails and trimmed it with the scissors, then realised he had cut it too short, and after ordering the little girl to be still, since she was already beginning to get restless, he trimmed the other one, making the same error of judgement yet again.

When they left the park, the ladies found Rasmi locked in gloomy silence and Zelda sobbing. Only a few wisps of hair poked out of the little white bows, the rest of the lovely copper-blonde mane lay on the gravel, reduced to tiny shreds.

As soon I had a chance to talk to Stiler alone I told him

about the extraordinary resemblance I had discovered between Artemis and Zee.

'Well done, Bausa, better late than never,' was his response. 'I noticed it at once, last summer, seeing Zelda again after all those years. You know, the last time we had met she was little more than a child, and she didn't look a bit like Artemis.'

'It's really an odd coincidence.'

'Quite, very odd. If there was any room in my mind for superstition . . .'

'You don't have to be superstitious to be struck by such an occurrence. It seems as if some higher will had preordained it all.'

'Every once in a while that's my impression too. But of course there is a less absurd explanation: it's possible that when I looked at Zelda as a child I already had some inkling of how her adult physiognomy would be, and so, choosing the statue . . . You don't seem convinced, my dear friend.'

'Perhaps because this kind of explanation fails to satisfy my incurable tendency to romanticism. The idea of a miracle is much more interesting.'

'You are greatly mistaken: a miracle is always the most banal solution, I'd say almost a quick way out for someone who doesn't want to think about things too much. To say nothing of the fact, Bausa, that miracles don't exist, at least as far as I'm aware.'

'That seems to me a rash conclusion of yours.'

'In that case, I shall leave you free to believe what best pleases you. Weave whatever web of fantastic conjectures you like around that resemblance, have your fill of puzzling over fate or divine providence. As for me, if you don't mind, I prefer to stick to logic.'

This parade of rationality did not convince me: he too had certainly found some kind of omen in this strange link between Artemis and Zee, and I was sure that this, at least partly, was at the root of his infatuation with the young woman. All the same, I realised, it would have been impossible to make him admit it.

'They are both perfect, my friend,' Stiler went on, 'but in Zelda there is something more: in her there is life in addition to perfection, and the supreme form of life, that of the spirit, while Artemis is just inert matter.'

'Thank you. I venture to presume that the difference between a statue and a flesh and blood woman would not have escaped me even without you taking the trouble to clear it up, however . . .'

'Your sarcasm, Bausa, is misplaced. The disconcerting phenomenon is precisely that a flesh and blood woman should have the perfection of a statue, as if Artemis had come down from her pedestal and were walking about in the garden. Do you see, absolute beauty *plus* life: this, you must acknowledge, is almost a miracle.'

'A miracle? But wasn't this the very suggestion that you were repudiating with such vehemence?'

'Come, come, don't fool yourself that you've caught me out so easily. It's quite clear that I was expressing myself in a figurative sense.'

For a little while I was lost in thought. 'Absolute beauty plus life . . .' I said at last. 'I thought that life necessarily entailed some little chicken bone or other.'

'No Bausa, not necessarily. You only have to look at my cousin to realise that.'

It struck me that Stiler's deductions made him overlook

the freckle side a little too much, but I refrained from pointing it out to him.

At first, whenever I reached the villa, I would be amazed still to see the lightning-struck oak, with its dried-up branches and carbonised trunk, but as time passed I ceased to expect that Stiler would make up his mind to have it cut down. He too seemed used to it by now, or rather resigned to its melancholy presence; whenever we talked about it he would continue to restate his determination to get rid of it, yet he deferred the operation until some increasingly hazy future date.

It was clear that his attentions were being directed towards Zee and removed from the garden, for which he now had only hurried and absent-minded looks. For all that, this place did not seem in the least to elude the iron discipline imposed by its demiurge: the sole, glaring exception was precisely the lightning-struck oak which, however, though it displeased Stiler, enjoyed the compensation of being especially liked by his cousin, in whose eyes it appeared 'picturesque'.

The authoritativeness of this verdict gradually augmented as Zee, first jokingly, then with ever greater seriousness, assumed the manners and prerogatives of the mistress of the house. Instead of settling into her comfortable position as the idle guest, by a series of small imperceptible moves she had firmly taken control of household management, to the great satisfaction of Stiler, who thereby saw his own future happiness prefigured, and of Ursula too, who certainly had no regrets about being relieved of many responsibilities and being able once more to go to the village every day to gossip to her heart's content with the locals.

The yoke imposed by Zee was a light one, to which anyone would have been happy to submit, a conciliatory influence radiating from her person with the ineluctability of a star radiating light. And yet when I saw her wandering about the garden casting critical looks around I found myself with a sense of vague apprehension for Artemis: I already pictured the white goddess languishing neglected, relegated to the darkness of a lumber room, the sheen of her marble obscured by dust and cobwebs, while the big Zee of red blooms would have taken uncontested pride of place in the flower-bed, extending its ever more blatant dominion across the whole property. And however much I was charmed by the young woman, I felt compelled to side against her with that divinity whose icy form had once seemed so alien to me.

One day, on my way back up the main avenue, I became aware of something odd about my surroundings. Finally I realised that a faint twittering violated the silence in which the garden was usually plunged, and peering through the branches of the lightning-struck oak I saw a pair of sparrows flit past in search of some non-existent nourishment. Just yards away, Ursula watched them triumphantly.

'Do you see, sir?' she said when I reached her. 'They've come back at last.'

'I noticed, and soon the engineer will notice too.'

She shrugged. 'He already knows, and there is nothing he can do about it, thank goodness. He was on the point of running to get his rifle, I read it in his eyes, but the young lady was so clearly pleased about them being here that he had to resign himself and leave the rifle where it was.'

'So the birds now have free access to the garden?'

'Certainly, and it's all Miss Zelda's doing. I myself have always said that what the engineer needed was an angel like her as his companion.'

I omitted to remind her that she had always affirmed the exact opposite. 'It has a strange effect hearing the birds sing among this greenery after so long.'

'That's quite true, sir, it's as if we'd been freed of a weight. And then, look at how graceful they are: they give the garden that little something it lacked, a touch of life, of joyfulness.'

They were indeed graceful, and it comforted me that Zee had succeeded in ending the cruel persecution to which Stiler had subjected them, but that gay twittering, that 'touch of life' which so enthused Ursula, struck me as being in strident dissonance with the garden, as if two irreconcilable elements now had to co-exist. I remembered the theory which Stiler had set out for me during our last talk and I wondered whether life could represent a 'plus' in relation to absolute beauty or whether it did not inevitably entail its diminution.

Someone called out suddenly, taking my mind off these thoughts. I turned and saw Stiler coming towards me, followed by Zee who walked along the avenue at her usual indolent pace.

'Come into the house, Bausa,' he said as soon as he was near me, as if he was in a hurry to remove the lightning-struck oak from my sight, and the sparrows, whose flight seemed to express the brazen confidence of those who know they are protected by immunity.

145

But Zee, in her apparently accommodating style, obliged us to linger.

'Do go on, I'll stay here a bit longer. It's a splendid day, and it's lovely to be outside . . .'

Ursula rushed to back her up by offering to serve tea in the garden.

'What's it got to do with you?' retorted the engineer crossly. 'You will serve tea when and where you are ordered to do so.'

'Yes sir: so tell me, when and where.'

Stiler shot a glance at his cousin, who meanwhile had sat down at the little marble table and was watching the birds' acrobatics through the blackened branches. 'Didn't you hear?' he finally said to Ursula. 'The young lady wants to stay in the garden.'

The servant went off sniggering. Overcoming his private reluctance, Stiler sat down beside Zee and invited me to do the same.

'Those little birds are delightful, Rasmi. If I had a garden like this, I should build a great aviary.'

'An aviary?' he repeated, visibly relieved. 'Hmm, it's not a bad idea, on the contrary, it's certainly worth considering. Locked in a cage, at least the birds wouldn't be able to do any damage.'

'It would be a pity though; it's so lovely to see them at liberty . . . don't you find too, Daniele, that their being in the garden gives it . . .'

'A touch of life, of joyfulness.'

'That's exactly it. You took the words out of my mouth.'

Thanks to Ursula's mediations, as ever, it was not long

before these signs of the engineer's surrender became known to the village people, who drew the obvious conclusion that he had 'softened up'. Besides, they affirmed, he could well afford it by now: an inexorable order reigned there, the garden prospered, upholding its own decorous magnificence, so that nothing forbade its maker from allowing himself some distraction; and it was not really possible to imagine any distraction more pleasurable than the one supplied by Zee.

From this viewpoint, therefore, everything was plain as could be to them. What they could not grasp, however, was the reason why such a woman, who had doubtless no shortage of suitors, seemed to favour the company of this man who was older than her and who had such an unlovable nature into the bargain. They would have suspected her of ulterior motives, had the luxurious automobile not been quite enough in their eyes to render incredible any suggestion of a Zee impoverished and seeking a way out with a marriage of convenience. Moreover, even were this the case it would have been a peculiar choice: the engineer was comfortable, but not wealthy, and the life he would probably offer his bride in no way matched the natural aspirations of a young city lady. Those people, born and brought up in the countryside, were almost heartbroken at the idea that a creature like Zee might share their lot, that, in expiation of a temporary dazzlement, she would be condemned to spend the long winters among the snow-covered hills, far from any theatres or concerts, from the brightness of street lights and shop windows. A bitter fate, they said, awaited those garments of such elegance, those little hats in the latest fashion destined to be shown off only to an audience of sheep, hens and peasants, categories all equally ignorant of the rules of good taste, as arrived at by them, with laudable awareness of their own limitations, from their rare and bemused reading of some illustrated magazine or other which had chanced to end up on one of the café tables.

Unless, of course, the young lady managed to separate the engineer from the garden; but despite the softening up which by now, it seemed, had reached an advanced stage, a possibility of that kind was unanimously ruled out as a vain chimera. The ogre had certainly been able to entice the beauty into his lair; likewise he would know how to keep her there, with pitiless egotistical determination, and they were sure that not even when he had seen the young bride fade prematurely in that solitude, not even then would he take the step of moving to the city.

The manner in which the peasants painted this dark picture did not lack a certain hint of admiration, which could sometimes prevail over any impulse of compassion: for his resistance to the blandishments of the city, for his stubborn attachment to that place, they took the view that notwithstanding all the differences and incomprehensions, Stiler had become one of them, that he now belonged to the land to which they belonged and was its champion against anyone who dared to question its great worth. At such times they failed to remember that they had been the first to question it, or they deemed this an insignificant detail, so proud were they that someone should regard that 'godforsaken' place as his own ideal abode, and when they recalled Zee in the light of these patriotic feelings they almost went so far as to rejoice in her probable sacrifice. That woman deluded herself about being able to triumph over one of them, about being able to soften him up enough to deprive him altogether of his will, but this case more than any other would bear out the profound truth of the saying that he who laughs last laughs best.

In obedience to Stiler's request, I had in the meantime made inquiries about hiring a piano, yet within only a few days I had been persuaded that this was an unrealisable project: not just our village, but also the small towns nearby seemed characterised by a complete absence of familiarity with the muses, nor was there even a trace of any shops where sheet music was sold; admittedly, there were rumours of the odd notable who owned a gramophone or a musical instrument, but the channels whereby they came into possession of them remained swathed in the most impenetrable mystery.

After having passed on the disappointing outcome of my researches to Stiler, I took no further interest in the matter, and thought that he too had totally dropped it. Instead, one afternoon, as I crossed the garden heading for the villa, I heard a slow, tender melody issuing through the open windows of the drawing-room, and entering on tiptoe I saw Zee absorbed in playing a black lacquered upright piano. Her mother and Stiler were both listening, she with an ecstatic expression, he with an air of indulgent toleration.

When she became aware of my presence, Zee broke off. 'Do you see, Daniele, Rasmi wanted to give me a surprise.'

'You might well say that he wanted to offer us all a great pleasure. But go on, I implore you.'

'Oh, they were just little exercises to stretch my fingers,' she replied, hiding her satisfaction under a display of modesty. 'I don't intend to take advantage of your good manners.'

Finally, however, she yielded to my pleas and began playing again, while I settled into an armchair. She performed several pieces one after the other, her choice mirroring a conception of music that bore the imprint of refined hedonism; listening to her one was really tempted to believe that the genuine essence of art could be reduced to a capacity to provoke a particularly elevated kind of pleasure, to give life an aesthetic completion that was in total harmony with its requirements, and that the search for any other meanings in it was merely a pointless complication.

I listened to her explore the complex interweaving of themes in a sonata movement with an expert touch, and my thoughts went back to the defence of tortuousness which she had one day opposed to Stiler's strenuous rationalism. All of a sudden I realised that the meaning of that defence did not lie, as it did for me, in the perception of finding oneself in a labyrinth where one is continually exposed to the risk of losing one's way or even of bumping into a minotaur. No, nothing so dramatic: in Zee's eyes tortuousness was more like a drapery in which things were mantled so as to increase their fascination, and, with untroubled grace she could penetrate these rich folds and sinuous lines, this softness of light and shade, without the least presentiment of its possible snares.

And yet her style could not be described as superficial.

Her delicacy of touch, her extremely fine instinct for nuance, saw to it that the enchantment of the senses which it created was supplemented so much as to become an enchantment of the spirit. Her mother was certainly wrong, Zee did not play at all like an angel: if when listening to her there were times when one felt one was in Paradise, it was however a different Paradise, in no way ascetic, where obliging houris offered all the sweetness of earthly existence.

From time to time I turned towards Stiler, but very quickly I noticed that, although he maintained a mask of superior detachment, he was so absorbed in the music that he could not respond to my look; it seemed that hearing his cousin play aroused in him, almost against his will, an intense emotion.

'From what I see,' I said to him when Zee had shut the piano lid, 'music irritates you less than usual today.'

'My nephew has always been like that: when he talks, it amuses him to pose as being impervious, but in fact . . .'

Stiler did not reply; all he did was cast Zee a long glance of approval which probably was not only in reference to her gifts as a performer.

As soon as I had a chance to talk to him privately, I asked him where he had managed to get hold of that piano.

'It wasn't easy, my friend; but as you know, I am not in the habit of giving up. In any case it was worth the trouble, my cousin is so pleased . . .'

'I fear though that I disturbed her; perhaps in front of a stranger . . .'

'In the first place, Bausa, you are in no way a stranger, and in the second place, I know for sure that

Zelda sets particular store by your opinion. Indeed, she will certainly appreciate it very much if from now on you will come regularly to hear these little performances.'

'I should be very glad to.'

'I have no doubt of it. If I'm not mistaken, you were the music lover.'

And so, in the days that followed, I became accustomed to turning up at the villa in time to applaud our houri in the guise of pianist. The manner in which she played enabled me to increase my understanding of an essential trait in her character which until then I had not had the means to grasp: a blind, even moving faith in the inevitable triumph of a tranquil and moderate joy, such that it impelled her to perform the most troubling passages without taking them seriously, as if the pain they reflected were only a rite of passage placed on our path by some benevolent pedagogue so as to let us fully relish our re-found serenity. And it was to the latter that she abandoned herself in the most complete and voluptuous way, so devoid of the slightest reserve that I could not help myself from envying her: life, I thought, rewards its most devoted children by giving them a limpid mind, inaccessible to every deep disquiet.

Once, nearing the villa, I noticed that the friezes and trompe-l'oeil pilasters shone through the paint work: the whitewashed facade was animated by ghostly tints, by a dawning of faintly outlined forms. I wondered whether it had merely been absent-mindedness that had stopped me from discovering it sooner, or whether instead the old ornamental motifs had gradually reemerged through the coat of paint that hid them and only now had become visible.

As I stood on the central avenue looking at this singular phenomenon, I was joined by Ursula.

'Good evening, sir. Are you admiring the view?'

I pointed to the facade, and she too, looking closely, was able to make out those pale friezes.

'It's really strange. The engineer had them give it four coats, and the old mural was already so discoloured . . .'

'And yet it has reappeared. Could it be that the engineer has seen it?'

'I doubt it, sir: for some time now all he has seen is . . . a certain person.'

'We ought to tell him about it, don't you think?'

'If we tell him about it, he will give instructions to re-paint the facade; I'd stake my life on it.'

'Naturally. Why ever shouldn't he?'

'Because it's better like this, in my modest opinion. With that little bit of colour, it has a less gloomy look.'

'White, Ursula, isn't a gloomy colour.'

'If you say so . . . It has always made me feel sad; but I am just a poor ignorant woman. I make no pretence at knowing how to judge these things.'

Thinking back on the roses of all different colours that adorned the outside of her house, I realised how much she must have disliked the sight of that mono-chrome surface. Undoubtedly, the reappearance of the friezes and pilasters in her eyes represented a reconquest of variety and beauty over the rigid uni-formity imposed by Stiler.

'For the time being, Ursula, I think it's pointless to talk to him about it. He certainly won't be able to have the wall re-painted until his guests have gone, and besides, as you yourself remarked, at the moment he is almost entirely engaged with matters of quite a different sort.'

'Yes, sir, best to leave things as they are. Sooner or later, alas, he'll end up noticing it by himself.'

However, in the days that followed, he did not appear to notice it at all, and I kept silent about my discovery: some obscure protective instinct forbade me from revealing it to Stiler, but I could not have said what it was that I wanted to protect, whether it was that particularity of the villa in the past, miraculously restored to my sight, or the engineer's serenity, which would undoubtedly have been upset by so underhand a rebellion. When I went along the central avenue and saw the lightning-struck oak and the pale touches of colour on the facade of the house, I too felt a vague anxiety, even though the harmony with which Stiler had imbued the garden prevailed over those small signs of disorder.

Up there, meanwhile, life proceeded in the usual way. Even though the engineer showed himself daily more yielding towards her wishes, Zee did not seem satisfied: the piano and the little walks were not enough to dissipate the boredom which that monotonous life and immutable landscape inspired in her, and the incidents and dramas caused by atmospheric shifts and the progress of the seasons were almost imperceptible to her distracted gaze. With countless excuses, Stiler went on refusing to absent himself from the garden for very long; Ursula's husband had even stopped looking after his automobile, whose bodywork was now covered by a dense layer of dust and dried-up leaves.

In the course of a talk which I now experienced as

something in the distant past, Stiler had solemnly affirmed to me that he wanted to find a solution, not a compromise, but from my observations of how his relationship with his cousin had developed I had to acknowledge that he had not kept faith with this intention. What had been established at the villa was quite patently a compromise, one possessing however the bizarre characteristic of proving unsatisfactory for both parties; it was a life for octopus or crayfish, to which Stiler would once have firmly refused his approval, deeming it unworthy of a rational being. Now however he submitted to it without protest, yet in Zee's eyes his personality continued to appear opaque, tarnished, inexplicably different from that of the brilliant man she had spent time with in town.

One evening, arriving at the villa shortly before dinner, I found her alone in the drawing-room. She was idly leafing through a magazine with the air of someone who has to sit and take her turn in a waiting-room. The moment she saw me she put the journal down and in a tone of jocular indignation announced that everyone had deserted her: her mother would not cut short her afternoon nap, and the engineer had shut himself up in his study to get on with some urgent correspondence. I at once offered myself as a remedy for that lack of gallant conduct: if she would allow me to take Stiler's place, I should be very glad to accompany her on a walk. She accepted, left the room and some minutes later returned wearing a broad-brimmed hat whose shade hid her face like a little veil.

We set out beneath a sky thick with clouds which seemed from on high to extend that seige laid by the hills. Zee too was clouded, and more taciturn than

usual. I suggested that we go around the house towards
her flower-bed, but she appeared altogether unenthusi-
astic about this idea. 'Do we absolutely have to stay in
the garden? I thought that we could push on a bit
further away.'

'As you prefer.'

'I hope you won't judge me too harshly,' she said,
when we were on the other side of the gate, 'if I confess
to you that I cannot share Rasmi's passion for this
place.'

'Why should I judge you harshly?'

She stopped and gave me a long look. 'That's good.
In any case, I wouldn't even have mentioned it had I
not known I should find you an understanding listener.
I should like you to be my friend, Daniele,' she added
in a quieter voice.

All of a sudden I felt myself to be in danger, as if
with those words Zee had shaken the high observation
tower where I had taken refuge. Nonetheless I kept
control of myself and gave her the answer she expected:
'I don't think I have ever given you reason to doubt
my friendship.'

'No, in fact, I have never seriously doubted it. You
are a friend of Rasmi, and therefore you are a friend of
mine. The two things are closely connected, even if at
times it might seem . . . But I'm talking too much this
evening, and perhaps I'm boring you.'

She had expressed this scruple only so that I could
proclaim it to be groundless, which I at once did, urging
her to go on.

'Help me out, Daniele: what were we saying?'

'You were saying, and rightly so, that the engineer's
friends are necessarily your friends.'

'Yes, quite so, because all I wish for is what is right for my cousin. Whereas I'm not altogether sure that he knows what is right for him. In this case however there would have to be someone to help him find out, don't you think? And this is exactly what friends are for, if I'm not mistaken.'

The shocks, the sense of danger, had become more violent. With these allusive words, Zee wanted therefore to compel me to take her side, she wanted me to back her up in her attempt to separate Stiler from the garden. Under the wing of shade cast by her hat, those eyes which were usually so veiled seemed extraordinarily bright, and their gleam was fixed once more on me, steady and penetrating, as if to probe me or to conquer me.

I pretended suddenly to be interested in a flowering shrub which spread its foliage on one side of the avenue. I picked a flower and offered it to Zee. Silently, without interrupting her scrutiny of me, she slipped it into the neck-line of her dress.

'Perhaps we should go back,' I said, 'it's almost time for dinner.'

We set out, and since Zee remained silent, after a little while I added, involuntarily assuming an apologetic tone: 'Whatever the case, I think the engineer has no need of advice, he can work out for himself what is right for him.'

'That may be, but to see a man of such stature give up any serious profession, any ambition . . .'

'On the contrary, I am convinced that in these last few years your cousin has cultivated a very great ambition.'

'Devoting himself to gardening?' she answered with

a forced smile. 'You astound me, Daniele, I considered you to be more reasonable.'

'I am even too much so: I do not in fact devote myself to gardening.'

We were already within sight of the villa, and instinctively we quickened our pace so as to terminate that conversation all the sooner. In the hallway we parted, taking our leave with a certain coldness; I observed that Zee no longer wore the flower I had given her, she must have thrown it away along the road. She went up to change for dinner, while I joined Stiler in the drawing-room. When we met again at table, she smiled to show me that she bore no grudge, and during the meal we both strove to hide the crack which had opened up in our relations. Already between Zee and Stiler too all topics which might have given rise to disagreement had been barred for some while, but now that circumspection, that artful concordance made me uneasy, so that I felt relieved when at last the time came to say goodnight. The relationship between the two cousins, I reflected as I walked down to the village, had undergone a profound change: it was no longer based on mutual ignorance, as at the start, but on mutual incomprehension.

In the period that followed, Zee showed that she had no need of my help and succeeded in establishing a perfectly tranquil atmosphere, based on the unconditional surrender of her adversary; Stiler, I observed not without apprehension, seemed really to have altered, as if the presence of his cousin had little by little broken down his willpower. Now, with an unexpected meekness, he let himself be governed by her in all things, becoming with every day that passed more like the little dog on the leash conjured by the divinatory powers of the village, and as this metamorphosis was gradually completed, Zee's attitude became gayer and more affectionate.

Stiler's submissiveness reached the point where he was impelled to offer himself spontaneously to his cousin as her partner in those same checkers games which in better days he had kept out of, professing a proud contempt for such futile activities. Exhibiting infinite patience, he would wait for the woman he loved to make a move without taking the liberty of pressing her to stop dithering: all he did was shift about a bit in his chair to break the continuing immobility, while she weighed up every single move unhurriedly, as if she had all the time in the world, or else completely forgot about the game and launched into voluble conversation.

As for myself, I valued the positive aspects of this state of affairs, I was delighted to see Stiler's hopes close to fulfilment, and yet I could not manage to stifle a disappointment whose roots, honesty compels me to admit, were primarily egotistical. If for so long I had believed that I had won the friendship of an extra-ordinary individual, the privilege of watching a singular destiny unfold, now all I had left was an insipid love story, and the engineer's titanic enterprise had dwindled to the renovation of a country residence. How could my parasite nature draw sufficient nourishment from such ungenerous ground?

Nonetheless I was careful to hide this disappointment both from Zee, in whom an awareness of victory had intervened to erase any trace whatsoever of resentment towards me, and from Stiler himself. Since the day when the two guests had reached the villa, we had seldom had an opportunity to talk alone, and the more the engineer inclined to Zee's wishes, the more a veil of reserve was drawn over our relations, as if in me he feared an inclement witness. On the other hand, this very fear seemed for him to heighten the importance of my good opinion: whenever I addressed Zee with words of praise he would appear as happy as a child seeing his favourite toy approved by the teacher.

'Yes, Bausa, you're quite right,' he would say, touchingly assuming the tone of an expert concerned to formulate an impartial aesthetic judgement. 'She is a flesh and blood Artemis, there is no other way of describing her.'

He did not even mention the freckles any more, though these, thanks to the sunlight, were in a phase of notable efflorescence.

The two sparrows I had seen among the blackened branches of the oak did not remain an exception for long: very soon the garden, whose out-of-bounds status was no longer defended by the engineer's rifle, became populated with birds of every species, blackbirds and robins, swallows and crows, in ever greater numbers, as if in their eyes the former prohibition conferred a particular attraction on that place. Nor were the earthbound animals any fewer, who, furtively at first, then bold as brass, carried out repeated raids on Erasmo Stiler's property; a mole even had the temerity to tunnel under a flower-bed, ruining its compact surface with little hilly mounds of earth.

However much he was distracted by his love for his cousin, Stiler could not but notice this invasion, and he contemplated its effects with resigned bitterness.

'They're attacking me on all sides,' he said once during a walk in the garden. 'From the sky, from the earth...'

'They're attacking you?' Zee repeated laughing. 'Come on, Rasmi, don't exaggerate. All they're doing after all is seeking out their natural environment.'

'But this, dear Zelda, is *my* natural environment.'

She shrugged. 'There's room for everyone, it seems to me: these creatures aren't making a nuisance of themselves.'

'So long as they don't come into the house,' her mother stipulated. 'Especially the mice.'

'Fine, there's room for everyone,' Stiler muttered in a gloomy tone, and quickly changed the subject.

It was clear that he too grasped that incongruity which I had noticed in the garden since the day I saw the sparrows fluttering around the oak, that intrusion of life into a place dedicated to immobility, but he made the effort to believe that the two opposing laws could co-exist without mutual violation. And whereas he was abandoning his once rigid vision, I on the other hand felt myself impelled to adopt it, to perceive what surrounded me in the same way that he had perceived it before he succumbed to Zee's charm.

It was even painful for me to look at the garden while she played, to imagine that music spreading like a rosy sentimental cloud over the rigorous geometry of the flower-beds and enveloping everything, including the statue of Artemis. I wondered whether the goddess could still breathe in such an alien atmosphere, or whether she was doomed to be gradually crushed by her fleshly twin, who with ever superior strength exerted her own suave poison.

During the same period when the animals installed themselves anew, other symptoms of anarchy appeared in the garden: weeds of a particularly stubborn variety sprouted here and there, persisting however much they were rooted out, a fact which Stiler attributed on the one hand to the gardener's lack of experience, on the other to the perfidy of the birds bringing the seeds inside the confines of his property, from the hills, where plants like these grew in abundance.

All of this was probably true, and yet it struck me that those apparently insignificant phenomena were harbingers of a deeper evil. The bond between Stiler and his work of creation had now split, perhaps irremediably. It was not just a matter of weeding the flower-beds; for the garden to go back to being the way it was before, the engineer would once more have had to consecrate his attentions, his thoughts, his whole life to it, with that unconditional dedication of which he no longer seemed capable.

However irritating they proved to be for him, the proliferation of little chicken bones was not enough to make him change his outlook. The nearness of Zee fogged everything else, beside her the engineer was being transformed, from the defiant figure with no background whom I had once drawn, into a normal man, for whom nothing would stand in the way of relishing family joys nor accomplishing that precious contentment which was achievable only through a mediocre existence.

The poet of coldness was trying to warm himself in

the glow of a domestic hearth, and it was so blatant a thing that it did not even escape the village people's notice. The respect this unusual person inspired in the café regulars was being extinguished, since it was no longer permissible to harbour the slightest doubt about his conclusive 'softening up'; the women made up for this whenever they met in the square on market day by predicting with satisfaction the imminent happy ending of this exemplary series of events whereby love once more demonstrated what power it has, already amply illustrated by novels, to turn bad people into good and make everyone live happily ever after.

The day came at last when Stiler made up his mind to spell out his plans to me. It was early on a baking hot afternoon, and the ladies were resting in their bed-rooms: I had remained in the drawing-room with him, keeping him company as he smoked his post-prandial cigarette and trying to stir his interest in a wide range of conversational topics even though it was patently directed elsewhere. However, when I desisted from those vain attempts and was on the point of saying goodbye, he suddenly roused himself and solemnly asked me to allow him a few more minutes.

'It happens so rarely, dear Bausa, that I can talk to you man to man, so to speak, just between ourselves . . . You've seen quite a lot of my cousin by now, so you must have formed a pretty clear opinion of her.'

I was about to answer, but Stiler forestalled me: 'Let's be plain, I don't want you to go into it; in the first place it would be superfluous, given that I've already got my own, and in the second place it would be disrespectful towards Zelda.'

'I don't see why. I think that on other occasions I've already expressed an unreserved admiration for your young guest.'

'I thank you, Bausa, but that is not the point. What I would like to talk to you about . . . is a very different matter.' He stopped short, got up from his armchair and went to the window, so that he had his back to me. 'You will doubtless have realised,' he continued, 'that my affection for Zelda is more intense than anything justified by a family bond. You will have realised, in other words, that I think of her not as a cousin, but rather . . .'

He fell silent, still not facing me, preferring that I be the one to finish the sentence mentally.

'Dear engineer Stiler, this is really wonderful news.'

He turned towards me again. 'I'm glad to hear you say so. Besides, as you know, Zelda and I have no blood relationship, so there is nothing to prevent us . . . nothing.'

'It would seem that you've considered the question in every respect.'

'It goes without saying, Bausa, that before reaching a decision of such gravity one must carefully weigh up every likely consequence.'

'Gravity, weigh up . . . This is a rather strange choice of words: I thought that an engagement, for all its seriousness, was a joyful event, to be confronted with a more serene disposition.'

'Engagement? You're going too fast. For now, all that I have conveyed to you is my intention. I am reasonably certain that it will find a favourable reception, however...'

'You mean that you haven't yet conveyed it to Zelda?'

'Exactly. You may well maintain that I should have done so before mentioning it to you, and I acknowledge you are right, but I was anxious to have your sincere opinion.'

'My opinion?'

'Not of Zelda, I repeat. Merely... about whether it's a fitting step to take.'

'So you're not sure about it?'

'On the contrary, I'm absolutely sure.'

'In that case, act accordingly.'

'Thank you, dear friend, I shall do just that. You see, sometimes I suspect I'm no longer able to think of anything but my own happiness, neglecting there-fore... But if you too judge... After all, matrimony can be perfectly reconciled with the pursuit of other goals, indeed, it can actually favour them.'

'Without a doubt.'

'Naturally, when I have obtained, as I hope, Zelda's consent, there will still be a lot of details to clarify. For example,' he added, slightly lowering his voice, 'we would have to decide where to live.'

These words disconcerted me: I was yet to consider the possibility that Stiler would abandon the garden.

'I'm afraid that Zelda would not like living in the country,' the engineer continued. 'Moreover, as you know, I've never liked it either: I had to make a great effort to force myself to move here, and perhaps now the moment has come to make the opposite effort.'

'Are you really proposing to leave this house?'

'We'll see, Bausa, we'll see. In any case, I will not allow my property to go to rack and ruin: even if I had to move to town, I should come here very often to reassure myself that everything was in order.'

'And you would spend your holidays here, with your wife?'

'I beg you not to judge me too harshly.'

'I'm not judging you at all. You have every right to seek your happiness wherever you think fit.'

'What you say is an incontrovertible truth,' he replied, without paying any attention to the coldness with which I had uttered it. 'It seems to me that in recent years I've been living in a state of continual coercion, but now, thank heavens, I've managed to free myself. Because after all, being free means precisely having the power to seek one's own happiness wherever one wants.'

'I can't see what else it might mean.'

'You have no idea, dear Bausa, what a relief this conversation has been for me. Wherever one wants, it's obvious: or else are we trees, have we roots instead of feet?'

A few days later, on my arrival I found Stiler waiting for me at the gate with a distinctly dejected expression.

'What's the matter, engineer?' I asked in concern.

'Come with me, please: there's something I have to show you.'

Maintaining a gloomy silence, he led me to the semi-circular flower-bed. The moment I set eyes on them I perceived that many of the red flowers which made up the big Z were withered, as if some blight were slowly but surely draining them of all vital energy from inside; I could make out small dark spots here and there on the leaves.

'I've been an idiot, a fool. I should have noticed sooner.'

'Is it a serious disease?'

'Perhaps not, if treated in time; but I was too busy playing checkers. I haven't said anything to Zelda yet, so as not to upset her; you are well aware how fond she is of her flower-bed.'

'Yes, engineer, I know, and there is after all some chance of saving it. The majority of the flowers still look healthy to me.'

Instead of answering, Stiler bent down and picked one of them, breaking its stem, then he showed it to me: inside it was completely blackened.

'So there is nothing more that can be done?'

'There's always something that can be done, Bausa,' he retorted with a profound tiredness in his voice. This challenge, grave though it was, did not seem to have aroused his customary fighting spirit.

'Well then, let's try,' I urged him. 'Can I be of help to you in any way?'

'The diseased plants need to be rooted out and then burnt, so as to preserve the rest from contagion. But it's probably too late, the rot will have spread by now. If only I'd noticed in time . . .'

'You're not planning to stand by and do nothing to stop this destruction.'

'Certainly not: I've given the gardener all the necessary instructions, and they will be carried out today at the latest. Come, Bausa, it's time to join the ladies.'

As we had tea in the drawing-room, Stiler's eyes and

mine often turned to the windows, where occasional clouds of smoke would pass borne by the breeze. Zee and her mother were so absorbed in conversation that they took no notice.

I finally made my goodbyes, and when I was alone I did not head directly for the gate but went around the house to the back. In one corner, a little way from the flower-bed, was a heap of ashes; in the grass the big Z was broken up by glaring empty spaces and its contours appeared more irregular, though the shape was still clearly recognisable. The gardener was staring at it with a satisfied expression.

'Everything is fine now, sir; the plants that are left are healthy, every last one of them.'

This news prompted an access of relief that even then I regarded as disproportionate. Stiler had therefore committed the sin of being over-pessimistic: the garden's capacity for resistance was far greater than he thought, its will to survival much more tenacious. As I walked down to the village I wondered why the engineer had deemed that battle lost from the outset. Despair had never taken hold of him, yet now he had yielded to it with a certain morbid satisfaction, just as in some novels criminals tortured by remorse submit to their punishment. Perhaps, seeing the flower-bed restored to health he might even feel faintly humiliated, might have a sense of his own diminished importance.

The next day Stiler triumphantly informed me about the successful outcome of the disinfection operation, and I was ashamed of my nasty speculations.

'My dear friend,' he said, 'I have never been so happy to be wrong. All we have to do now is replace the little plants that are missing and everything will be as before.

Zelda will be happy too when I tell her about the danger her flower-bed has escaped from.'

The relief however was short-lived: a few days later the flowers became diseased again, the corollas were withered and drooped from the stems within which that strange blackish sap still ran.

'It really is the end now,' muttered Stiler, 'the only thing left is to root out all the plants.'

'What a pity,' was Zee's bland comment beside the wrecked flower-bed.

'I'll re-plant them, I promise you, as soon as the soil is healthy again.'

'Whatever you want, Rasmi, but you mustn't vex yourself about it; in the end, it's the thought that counts.'

'I imagined you liked those flowers.'

'Of course I liked them. Did I ever say I didn't?'

I was listening to them, and I was finding it increasingly difficult to understand why those two were attracted to one another. It remained the most likely theory that Stiler loved Zee because she resembled Artemis and that Zee reciprocated to keep faith with her childhood passion: a somewhat unsatisfactory theory, with which my intelligence took offence. If life used such risible causes in impelling men and women to unite their destinies, then I did well to stand aloof, far from the edge, without ever giving up my role as spectator. Any other choice, I thought, would represent degradation for a right-thinking human being, and I was amazed that Stiler of all people did not realise this, and instead was gobbling up his little chicken bone with dull-brained beatitude.

However, this was perhaps the result of a more

fundamental blindness: he had always had the illusion that he could dodge chance without sacrificing action, that he could transplant his own inner necessity into the very soil of chance, and often as I looked at the garden I had been forced to acknowledge that he had succeeded; now, though, everything on which I laid eyes, the lightning-struck oak and the flower-bed with its blackened blooms, the re-emerging friezes and the mole hills, all seemed to me to proclaim his failure. Now, I thought, the most dignified decision he could make would be to leave with Zee for once and all, to seek elsewhere the modest happiness to which he aspired. Here it would be out of place, like the weeds or the sugary arpeggios on the piano.

This kind of intransigence was thoroughly at odds with my temperament, but at that time I judged Stiler's actions and feelings in accordance with the criteria which he himself had set, pronouncing my pitiless verdicts on the basis of the laws established by him. I identified myself so radically with this perspective that gradually I conceived an out-and-out hostility towards Zee, which was heightened rather than attenuated by the attraction which that woman still continued to exert upon me. Indeed I felt this hostility flare up within me when I saw Zee so unperturbed and indifferent in relation to the devastated flower-bed, yet my rage was most of all directed towards Erasmo Stiler, the owner of the garden, who was wanting in his duties for the sake of an ill-advised passion. And in part what made me particularly unbending was the fanaticism of youth, the profound indignation of one who persists in the belief that life can be lived with unerring observance of one's own principles.

Later on I would have regarded these events differently and the resemblance to Artemis would not have struck me as the sole, absurd reason for Stiler's love of his cousin. I would have understood how what seduced him were precisely the aspects of Zee's personality which made her infinitely remote from him: her indolence, her thoughtlessness, her trustful surrender to those very forces which he had always opposed. Then I would have remembered indulgently, even fondly, his attempt to replace the gelid marble goddess with a more propitious and accessible divinity.

When they learned of the blight with which the flowerbed had been stricken, the inhabitants of the village did not hesitate to blame Zee. The accusation was founded on the straightforward reasoning that before her arrival everything was going well in the garden: if the situation had altered, if the plants were becoming diseased, if parasites and weeds prospered, the cause of such havoc could only be the presence of that elegant young lady.

They did not take the trouble to ascertain how she might have brought about such adverse effects, merely invoking the widespread dictum whereby frailty thy name is woman, a dictum of which both history and their direct experience furnished innumerable proofs. Regarded from this viewpoint, Stiler's cousin was just the latest, on a more modest scale, in that long line of negative heroines which was initiated by Eve, continued with Helen of Troy and in the course of the centuries drew into its ranks such alarming individuals as Cleopatra, Salome and the pharmacist's sister.

The unanimous recognition of this truth had the

power to erase from their hearts any trace of the sympathy which had been felt for the young woman until a short time before: if fate really had compelled her to live up there for ever, confined to the engineer's property, it would not have been she who suffered the worst of it, so much as the property itself, for a wife who cannot make herself useful is inevitably a hindrance, getting in the husband's way, disturbing his work, pestering him with her caprices. And how could a creature brought up in the lap of luxury and accustomed to the most absolute idleness not be capricious?

Of course, the person in question was a 'real lady', but precisely this circumstance, which at the start had filled them with a kind of petrifying wonderment, dissuaded them from ascribing to her those domestic virtues upon which rested the value of a wife, in their opinion somewhat more than on aesthetic or worldly qualities, and therefore, in the final analysis, the very success of a marriage. For it is true that frailty thy name is woman, but it is also true that this rule knows happy exceptions. In other words, the eternal feminine is not only represented by Salome or charming and unserviceable creatures like Zee; fortunately there also exists a different species, equipped with skilful hands and robust practicality, a species of which the late lamented bride of the baker had been the most outstanding example in man's memory. Such women surely could be found even in the more elevated classes; were that not the case, they reasoned, these would have died out long before now. And his neglect to procure one of these for himself, they concluded with a grave shake of the head, was no tribute whatsoever to engineer Stiler's foresight.

It was already late September, but the weather remained peculiarly mild. It seemed that summer had decided to prolong its stay in this part of the globe out of special regard for Stiler's guests, and the only sign of its waning was a softening of the light, which was made thinner by a faint mistiness.

While the engineer continued devoting almost all of his attention to Zee, the symptoms of revolt multiplied in the property. Anarchy triumphed, with every day that passed, giving the garden an increasingly similar appearance to the hills with which it was surrounded, and the boundary marked out so furiously by Stiler was becoming ever more unclear. He devised feeble attempts to stem the disorder, entrusting their execution to Ursula's husband, but with no results: in the now flagrant extravagance, in the seditious attitude with which that formerly so docile vegetation opposed all efforts to re-install the customary discipline, it seemed as if a wilful and indomitable force was taking its revenge on whoever had falsely imagined he could subjugate it.

Now the garden recalled for me again the wild place of old: hedges and bushes took advantage of Stiler's distraction to deviate, at first imperceptibly, then with growing affrontery, from the geometric forms in which he had constrained them, coarse tufts of grass erupted at intervals through the layer of gravel covering the pathways, and even the creepers had re-assumed their slow ascent of the villa's walls.

Stiler spent most of the time skulking indoors and would look out through the windows as if through the loop-holes of a besieged fortress. He would greet the bulletins of rout brought ever more frequently by

the gardener with a sad gesture of stretching out his
arms as if intimating that he expected it, that things
could not have gone any differently, and at heart I was
compelled to acknowledge he was right. Sometimes I
thought of him as the hero of a fairytale who in
exchange for the love of a princess had consented to
give up the magic ring which assured him the power
to command the world in accordance with his plans.
Perhaps he already regretted all that he had lost, as he
passed idle and undisturbed days in a house that was
now welcoming, or perhaps, and it seemed to me more
likely, Zee's presence dulled him so much that it prevented him from noticing that defeat in all its gravity.

Ursula too must have become aware that her master
had lost the magic ring, because she no longer bothered
to make a show of even that ironic obedience behind
which her dissent had been hidden until then. When
she cleared the table she would put to one side the
leftovers for the animals she still kept in cages in her
'*boudoir*' without making any mystery of their destination; other creatures had been released and roamed
about blissfully under the engineer's nose.

As for the blooms in the big flower-bed, Stiler had
had them re-planted, but a week later they were dead
again; it seemed impossible to eliminate that blight, the
garden continued to make a firm stand against Zelda's
initial, and she herself, in an only half-joking tone,
habitually lamented the fierce enmity that place exhibited towards her. All the same I found myself
harbouring some doubts about the existence of such
enmity. Could it be, I thought, that this woman with
her lazy eyes, her face dotted with freckles, is really
the rival of Artemis, or might she not instead be the

unconscious accomplice of the secret will which has always smouldered in the garden beneath its apparent decorum, of the incontestable yearning which drives it back to primitive formlessness.

One day I found the engineer under the oak which had been spared by the lightning. Ivy had climbed all the way up the little stone table, patterning it with shadowy green veins; in his hands Stiler held a torn-off tendril.

'Come, Bausa, sit down. Are you amazed to see me here?'

'Amazed?' I repeated, pretending not to understand. 'Why should I be? It's such a beautiful day . . .'

'One can't close ones eyes to reality forever, don't you think? I needed to take stock of the situation.'

'And have you taken stock?'

He gave the ivy tendril one last look, then threw it away far into the grass. 'I've scoured the garden from end to end, I've inspected every flower-bed, every single plant. My God, how many . . . how many little chicken bones!'

'Yes, I too have remarked a few defects here and there for some time now. Perhaps the gardener is not carrying out his work as he should.'

'No, my friend, it's nothing to do with the gardener, and you know that very well.'

'And yet this strange phenomenon . . .'

'Strange, you say? It strikes me as altogether normal, a clear-cut logical outcome. Nature gets its revenge if we turn our back on it.'

'This is a specific period you're going through, you are understandably distracted by other matters; but once your private life is running on more settled lines . . .'

'Who knows. Perhaps the little chicken bones are destined to get the better of us, perhaps they're closer to the essence of things than we are with our calculations. Because, dear friend, the essence of things is disorder.'

'I'm astonished to hear you talk like this.'

'Really? Did you perhaps think that I wasn't aware of it? No, Bausa, I've always been aware of it: only, I'm tired now, I don't feel up to a fight any more.'

'You once assured me that you were more stubborn than any bush or tree.'

'But I also said, if I remember correctly, that form is an unnatural condition, and can be maintained only by force.'

'And what stops you from continuing to exercise this force?'

'You can see very well: my mastery was a sham, the illusion of a child who convinces himself he is a king because he has put a paper crown on his head. I only had to take my eyes off it . . . Besides, don't deny it, you too have always been aware of it. You must have regarded me as a madman right from the start, ever since that day you came across me hitting the trees with a stick.'

'It's possible, engineer, that your enterprise has always struck me as hopeless, doomed to failure sooner or later. But its beauty resided precisely in this.'

'No, Bausa, there is no beauty in defeat.'

'On the contrary, it's difficult for me to recognise it in victory.'

'Then you mustn't regard nature as beautiful: it

always wins. I would find it easier to give up everything than to accept this aesthetic of weakness you have.'

'I wouldn't call it weakness.'

'No? And how would you describe it?'

'Wisdom, dear engineer. If you aren't up to facing your enemy any longer, all you can do is take its lead. Some results can be achieved even by this route.'

Stiler smiled. 'Are you suggesting that I cultivate little chicken bones?'

'That you inquire into their laws, instead of imposing yours on them.'

'The law, my friend, exists uniquely as something brought about by man. It is arbitrary, artificial, and outside this artifice there is only the most total senselessness.'

'Or what seems so to us.'

'God, which is to say nothing?'

'Why not?'

He shook his head slowly. 'You'll never succeed in persuading me, Bausa; but for the first time, I confess, I feel that it would be a great comfort to be able to believe it.'

Autumn arrived, and Stiler's guests began to make mention now and then of their departure. The shadow of sadness cast by forthcoming separation made those days precious to us, as the daylight hours, ever shorter, assumed greater value in our eyes. But it was also pleasant to sit in the drawing-room in front of the fire lit there and watch from the windows while the early twilight fell on the garden, with the leaves and grass that shone in the slanting rays of the sun, and then make my way back to the village as it was already getting dark and the trees along the way took on alien and fantastic shapes.

During that period our walks were stimulated by an edge of adventure, by a new sense of challenge. Zee and her mother tackled them wearing light outer garments which rippled in the wind, animating those figures with the same tremulous movement that ran through the foliage. We advanced with our arms hugging our chests for protection, and even Zee's pace struck me as faster, as if the autumn air imbued her with unaccustomed vigour. Perhaps for this reason, or perhaps because the engineer had learned to modify his own speed, the two of them finally managed to walk side by side.

Now Stiler would willingly travel far from the garden, seeming actually relieved when we left the hollow and it disappeared from our view; then he would begin to chatter animatedly, in a sparkling vein which was clearly to Zee's liking. I alone realised that in fact the engineer was talking without saying a thing, carefully avoiding any expression of opinion whatsoever. All of a sudden he seemed to have conceived a deep mistrust of principles, of abstract ideas, a radical doubt about their capacity to touch upon the truth of things; his mind became lost in the chaos of details and anecdotes as in some never-ending labyrinth from which he was no longer able to find a way out.

This made it distressing for me to witness these displays of gaiety, and I was almost glad when, back on the other side of the gate, he would once more lock himself inside a dismal silence, crossing the garden with a quick stride and never looking around. The two women gave no sign of observing these abrupt changes of mood, yet they surrounded him with their attentions, and Zee addressed him always in the sweet, protective manner with which a particularly well-behaved boy is addressed.

I did not know whether the engineer would join her in town to spend the winter; he had as yet said nothing about it to me, but after the conversation under the oak tree I was convinced that he was now close to a parting from the garden, perhaps a definitive parting. Having recognised the failure of his enterprise, Stiler had nothing left to do but leave and seek consolation in his cousin's love. At least in this respect everything seemed to be proceeding wonderfully, and without a doubt Zee would know how to reward my friend for his sacrifice, even though, I was sure, she could not be aware of how momentous it was. In exchange she would offer him, had already offered him, that priceless treasure called normality, that unique fount of every earthly happiness. At times I deprecated so mediocre a conclusion, then however I would remember the tone of stifled regret with which the year before Stiler had described to me the Christmases of his childhood, and it was not in me to condemn him.

But if he left forever, would he abandon the garden or would he be banished from it, as from a jealous homeland which rejects an unworthy son? It was not without bitterness that I recalled having one day compared Zee's presence up there to that of Eve in Eden.

Often, when I went up the avenue leading to the villa, I would pause to look at the facade where the faint floral motifs mingled with the spirals traced by the creepers, and the twisted trunk of the oak, and the dense undergrowth which now descended from the hills to violate the boundaries of the property, and the garden increasingly appeared to me to resemble how it had seemed to me so often before the engineer's arrival, yet I never felt any impulse to draw it: in its luxuriance I now discerned a mocking intention, an intolerable cruelty.

The later the season advanced, the more Stiler's sadness became palpable. His silences were so frequent, melancholy darkened his eyes so often and in so patent a way, that Zee and her mother had also finally become aware of it. As I learned from some hints dropped by the latter, they concurred in attributing his mood to an unconquerable shyness which prevented him from declaring his love for his cousin and placed him in an increasingly distressing position as the date for their departure gradually approached. I expressed my general agreement, although in reality I could not share such an interpretation; it was enough to watch Stiler crossing the garden, or raising his eyes from his desk to the haughty figure of Artemis and then lowering them at once as his face contracted in a brief grimace of pain, to understand the suffering that afflicted him. To see him in this state provoked such deep resentment in me that it led me to reject Zee's every attempt to establish greater intimacy with a coldness barely mitigated by good manners. This woman had managed to have Stiler driven out of his earthly paradise; I would at least prevent her from expelling me from my inaccessible observatory.

Thus the days went by, in an atmosphere of suspense

and expectation, until the conclusive one, when Stiler unequivocally revealed his intentions to his cousin. Foreign as he was to any kind of sentimentality, he did it in an altogether singular manner, and in the presence of witnesses, but even though it was still not a question of the marriage proposal which the two women eagerly awaited, it was enough to dispel any uncertainty from their minds and mine.

We were gathered for lunch around the big oval table. The October sun suffused the sky with a pale light, as if dimmed, and yet Stiler had ordered the curtains to be drawn, perhaps so as not to be disturbed by the sight of the garden turned to wilderness. After the soup, as soon as Ursula had gone off to the kitchen with the empty plates, the engineer, who until then had seemed completely plunged in his thoughts, re-emerged from them suddenly, addressing Zee.

'I shall absolutely have to take a look at my automobile. It will certainly need an overhaul, given that it hasn't been driven all summer.'

'It's too long since it has been driven, dear Rasmi,' remarked the aunt.

'I'll make up for that now by using it very often,' Stiler answered her, without however taking his eyes off Zee.

Thus, in an indirect way, he had at last announced his decision to leave the garden and return to town. I glimpsed an exchange of satisfied looks between Zee and her mother; as for myself, I had to bow my head to hide the disappointed expression which doubtless had been etched on my face: at that moment, I realised, the conclusive capitulation of Erasmo Stiler was consummated, and although I had long regarded it as inevitable, all at once I saw that I had always cherished the obscure hope of a different outcome.

'Yes,' Stiler reiterated, perhaps fearing he had not been fully understood, 'I shall use it very often.' And to make himself quite clear, he added: 'There are a thousand opportunities in town. I'll bring it round to the front of the house today, and the first thing I'll do is order the gardener to give it a wash. However, I prefer to check the mechanical parts myself.'

'That strikes me as an excellent idea, Rasmi,' said Zee with a radiant smile. 'I'll come and keep you company while you are working.'

'So long as you don't get too bored . . .'

'On the contrary,' the aunt interjected on her behalf, 'she'll be delighted, and perhaps she can even be of some help to you: as you know, Zelda too knows a bit about automobiles.'

There and then I decided to take my leave immediately after lunch with some excuse or other, so that my presence would not get in the way of that mechanical tête-à-tête between Zee and the engineer.

We chatted on about this and that until the maid came in with a large covered tray and dished out onto each of our plates a yellowish and ragged lump of some sort, at the sight of which the engineer was immediately gripped by a violent indignation.

'What can you be thinking of, Ursula, serving this kind of thing at table? Look at the shape of these omelettes!'

'They are the same as usual, sir.'

'In any case, take them away: it's time you learned to do things properly.'

'Take them away? Are the ladies and gentlemen planning to go hungry, by any chance?'

'Be so good as not to argue.'

Ursula left the room, and for a little while none of us said a word. Stiler avoided the eyes of the two women, who were staring at him in perplexity.

'This time, Rasmi,' the aunt finally said, 'I'd say you've gone too far.'

'Forgive me. If you wish, I'll tell Ursula to bring the omelettes back.'

'That's not the point,' Zee interjected, 'it's that your fury is out of place. Ursula's slovenliness is hardly something new.'

'Well then, all the more reason; it's time to make some changes.'

'Does it have to be today, Rasmi?'

'I fear, engineer,' I said, 'that the woman is incorrigible.'

'No one is incorrigible. The fault is mine alone: I should have been more strict and more attentive. There's nothing that causes more damage than being inattentive.'

Stiler was probably not just thinking of Ursula when he uttered these words.

'Come, let's change the subject,' Zee interjected. 'After all, it strikes me as a negligible detail.'

'No detail is negligible, Zelda. From what you say, things should always be left as they are, without care for anything, not even to get rid of that vegetable monstrosity which has been screaming vengeance for months, so twisted and burnt up.'

'If you're referring to the oak tree, Rasmi, I find . . .'

'Yes, I know, you find it is picturesque.' He fell

silent, then in a calmer tone he added: 'But perhaps you're not mistaken, it's better to change the subject.'

'The trouble is,' said the aunt, 'that you are too stubborn. One has to be able to adapt to circumstances in life: for instance, when my poor husband passed away . . .'

'Yes, Mummy, you showed admirable courage then, but if you'll allow me, I find the comparison is out of proportion. What this comes down to is just a tree, or an omelette gone wrong.'

'One more reason. You see, Rasmi, the capacity for adapting is also measured by trivialities. You ought to learn from your cousin: she never loses her temper, she never flies off the handle.'

'There's nothing special,' parried Zee, 'about making virtues out of necessity. On the contrary, if I'm honest I have to say I can't even understand how people can act any differently. When you know something is inevitable, it's best to resign yourself; and when you know it's impossible, why persist in wanting it?'

Stiler slowly looked up at his cousin. 'And yet, there are some who maintain that there is a special beauty precisely in this.'

'In what, Rasmi?'

'In knowing one is doomed to defeat, and nonetheless . . . But it's of no account, you are right, of course.'

'Of course. I really can't see what beauty there can be in defeat. One can get a lot out of life, so long as one is able to be satisfied: only madmen are ignorant of their limitations and rashly embark on hopeless undertakings.'

Stiler did not answer. He rose and went over to one

of the windows. Through the crack in the curtains he looked at the garden plunged in the noonday light.

He returned to the table when Ursula came in to serve the cheese. He ate his unevenly cut slice without making any comment, but the efforts we all made to restore his good humour were in vain. Finally, somehow or other, that lunch came to an end, and Zee suggested a short walk in the garden.

'Go ahead,' said Stiler, 'I'll stay indoors.'

'Don't be so lazy,' retorted Zee, who had clearly decided from then on to display her future wifely thoughtfulness, as if at a dress rehearsal. 'It's a lovely day, and it will do you good to get some exercise in the fresh air.'

As usual, the engineer ended up yielding to his cousin's insistence and, frowning, he followed us to the front door. I remarked that I would accompany them only some distance and would then return to the village, where I had something to see to.

'Oh, it won't be a very long walk,' answered Zee. 'We shall want to get back soon too, to rest for an hour or so; we'll have a lot of work to do this afternoon.'

We went out. In the sky some clouds had suddenly thickened, and the uncertain rays of the sun shed a cold light on the garden, making its colours livid.

'I fear a storm is on the way,' I said, but Zee rejected this forecast almost with disdain. 'A storm today? No, you're mistaken: you shouldn't give in to pessimism for the sake of a few little clouds.'

We reached the artificial lake where a layer of leaves, turned yellow, floated, then we returned along the little avenue and headed for the back of the house. Zee was in an access of uncontainable high spirits, and walking along arm in arm with an increasingly gloomy Stiler, she looked around boldly, as if she were asking the garden to acknowledge her victory and bow to it. But I did not doubt that it had already acknowledged it: this was why it had taken on such a desolate, even spectral appearance. It seemed that every tree, every hedge, every blade of grass froze prematurely at the thought of the long lonely winter.

We finally came to the big flower-bed.

'You'll see, Rasmi, that my flowers will bloom again. We'll re-plant them next spring when we come back.'

Stiler nodded and walked on: he seemed to be in a great hurry to get back. As we walked past the flower-bed, all of a sudden he saw something and came to a halt, his eyes staring and his expression halfway between fury and dismay. Following the direction of his eyes, I became aware that he was staring at Artemis: a long brown worm was slowly climbing up the belly of the goddess.

The engineer took a step towards the statue, but suddenly stopped short and dropped the arm he had raised in a threatening gesture. 'Now let's go back to the house,' he said in a voice so low that I could scarcely hear him.

Zee's meteorological optimism turned out to be very well founded: the storm did not break; on the contrary, even the clouds that had veiled the sky very soon scattered, and the sun shone undisturbed for the whole afternoon. I however stayed in my room, filling my sketch book with doodlings; I was too uneasy to want to go out. My heart tightened with compassion every time I thought back to the state of mind in which I had left Stiler, his despairing resignation when faced with the outrage endured by Artemis. But by now, like the sky, Stiler's mood too must have cleared: I imagined him up there, absorbed in fixing up his automobile along with Zee, and I imagined that between them everything would be settled during those hours, during those very minutes. While, in the margin of the folio, I drew a female nude with a long snaking line across her belly, the two cousins were undoubtedly laying the foundations of their life together. And when I saw the setting sun through the windows, that sunset struck me as particularly ripe with meaning, since the day's completion was also that of Erasmo Stiler's destiny.

I had promised the engineer and his guests that I would return the following day for tea, so at five I set out again towards the villa. After the final curve in the road, I was surprised to find Stiler's automobile parked as ever beside the gate, its bodywork coated in the usual layer of dust and dead leaves. But my amazement reached its height when I looked through the bars and saw the lightning-struck oak lying on the ground. The figure of a woman, in which I immediately recognised Zee was regarding the felled tree from a few steps away, and she appeared tiny, almost touchingly so, beside that huge tangle of blackened branches. I called to her, but she gave no sign of having heard me; she turned her back on the oak tree, hurried off towards the house, and before I could reach her she had disappeared through the front door.

I in turn stopped beside the oak tree. The trunk had been sawn off, there was only a short stump left in the ground revealing the whorled rings. A little further away the leafless branches were heaped up like brushwood.

Bewildered, I asked myself why Stiler had chosen now of all times to have it cut down. Perhaps it was not sufficient to justify my conviction that something serious had happened up here, some sudden upset, and yet this idea had flashed through my mind with great force the moment I had glimpsed Zee beside the tree, and now it struck me as confirmed by the silence in which I found the villa plunged, a silence halfway between reticence and resentment; I had the impression that within it some secret torment was being brooded over, with no wish at all that outsiders be made privy to it.

I was still hovering on the driveway, when Ursula came out of the house wearing a hat and carrying a shopping bag. As she advanced towards me she shook her head with a pensive and faintly amused air, as if she were privately considering some bizarre event of whose reality she could scarcely convince herself.

'Are you going down to the village now, Ursula?' I asked her. 'I thought you would be busy getting tea ready.'

'There isn't much to get ready today, sir, and the engineer prefers to see to it himself. I don't think you'll find anyone but him, because the ladies are not feeling well.'

'They aren't feeling well? Both of them?'

'That's right, it's an epidemic and no mistake.'

'And yet only just now I saw Miss Zelda in the garden.'

'If she came out into the garden, it was because the engineer took himself into his office some while ago.

The young lady feels better right away when she knows she won't have to meet him.'

'What do you mean, Ursula? What has happened?'

'I'll gladly explain it to you, sir, if you will walk along with me for a bit.'

And so we made our way together towards the gate. As we passed the felled oak tree Ursula shook her head again, let out a deep sigh and, not content with this, added a 'well!' to express her own perplexity to the greatest possible effect.

'Yesterday,' she then said, 'the engineer and my husband sawed away at it the whole afternoon.'

'I thought the engineer planned to see to the automobile.'

'The young lady thought so too. You should have seen her, the way she looked out at the door every couple of minutes while he fussed around that tree, and she had a look in her eyes as she stared at him, but she didn't say a word, and the engineer didn't say a word either. Only, before he was back inside, she came looking for me in the kitchen: "Please, Ursula, tell the engineer that I'm upstairs resting. I shan't even come down for dinner: I hope you won't mind bringing it to me in my bedroom." I did mind, there I am with enough work already, but I kept it to myself. "Is the young lady not feeling well?", I asked her. She nodded, hardly moving her head at all, then she ran upstairs, and she has stayed there, and her mother has stayed there to keep her company, and the same thing happened today at lunchtime. That's a nasty illness, sir, I saw what it was right away: she won't get over it that quickly.'

'Probably,' I replied with scant conviction, 'the

engineer will apply himself to the automobile today or tomorrow.'

'I get the feeling he won't, sir: he has already given instructions to call someone from the village to take away the tree and dig up the roots, and he wants to oversee the work from start to finish, that's what he said. And after that he wants to weed the flower-beds, and exterminate the parasites . . . the long and the short of it is he'll be kept busy for a good while. There hasn't been another word about the car. In any case, what would he need it for?'

'I must say, Ursula, I wasn't expecting anything like this.'

'With his Lordship you never know what to expect. And the thing is he's been behaving strangely ever since yesterday, you only have to think of how he attacked me when I served the omelettes. Don't be telling me it's normal, getting all worked up like that over such silliness.'

'Not usually, but in the case of the engineer . . .'

'And yet lately he seemed to have found some sense. Huh, obviously he can't help himself.'

'Yes, he can't help himself.'

We had reached the other side of the gate by now, and I decided to continue with Ursula as far as the village; I would send a note with my apologies for having missed that visit which would probably have been received with embarrassment by all the occupants of the villa. After such crucial hours, Stiler undoubtedly did not feel like receiving guests, and I myself was conscious of the need to unravel in solitude the knot of contradictory feelings which had become tangled up in my mind the more I listened to the housekeeper's story.

That night again I slept fitfully. As I drowsed I kept seeing Zee standing in front of the great oak, and I felt myself to blame as if I had become the engineer's accomplice in committing an act of cruelty towards her. Latterly, I told myself, I had wholly taken the side of Artemis, scarcely bearing in mind that the garden's rival was not in fact the incarnation of an abstract principle, but a living creature, capable of suffering.

Now however, this was in my mind, and I pictured quite vividly those dismayed glances cast at her cousin from the door and the curt phrases addressed to Ursula to cover up her wounded pride before Zee took refuge in her bedroom. But for all that I pitied the young woman, I understood the implicit meaning of Stiler's action and approved it without reserve. It must have been even harder for the engineer to sleep than it was for me, his silent affliction even deeper than that shown by Zee, yet he had acted in the only possible way.

I recalled what he had said to me one day about the necessity for choices and renunciation if one wishes to create works that are not fragmentary, the necessity to sacrifice any personal harmony and fulfilment so as to give harmony and fulfilment to the things which are entrusted to us. I was in agreement, even if perhaps I would not be capable of following him along that road; at least in theory I accepted the poetics of coldness with all its pitiless corollaries. Was perhaps the ruined state into which the garden had plunged not a demonstration that Stiler had been right? Yes, I repeated to myself, he had acted in the best way, in the only possible way.

And yet there appeared in my mind the recurring image of a glittering Christmas tree, surrounded by presents wrapped in brightly coloured paper, and I grasped what violence Stiler must have had to exert upon himself in order to push away that image, when he had made up his mind to devote himself to the garden and disappoint Zee's expectations.

We all met together again the next day. We were in the drawing-room, and at the piano Zee was picking out the notes of some of her favourite pieces, playing them with a distinct absence of warmth. The triumphs of joy were considerably less triumphal than usual, the caressing touch of the houri had given way to an almost severe stiffness, but the melodies served at least to mask the embarrassed silences which often arose between us. Sitting on the sofa, Stiler listened to her with his eyes riveted to his own knees.

'My aunt and my cousin,' he told me abruptly, 'intend to leave tomorrow.'

'Yes, Daniele,' Zee confirmed without stopping her playing, 'it's time we left. It's getting cold, and Mummy's health...'

'You're right,' said Stiler in a husky voice, 'the summer is certainly over.'

There was a long pause, then the engineer's aunt embarked upon a highly detailed description of her rheumatism, in which we all feigned to be deeply interested. 'This is why,' she concluded, 'my daughter has taken the wisest decision: if we were to stay in the country any longer, I would end up getting ill for sure.

I only hope that she doesn't mind too much that we're leaving.'

'Your health comes first, Mummy.'

Zee left the piano and went and sat down exactly opposite Stiler, who still kept his eyes lowered so as not to meet her gaze.

'I shall miss you,' the engineer finally said.

'Oh, I don't think so: the garden will be enough to keep you company.'

He did not reply.

'And you, Rasmi,' asked the aunt, 'how do you propose to spend the winter?'

'As always.'

'We shall see you in town, I hope.'

'I don't know, Aunt. I fear I shall have a lot to do here.'

Zee got up. 'Please do excuse me, it's time for me to go upstairs and pack.'

'I thought Ursula was taking care of it,' said Stiler.

'All the same I want to be there, so as to tell her what needs to be done. But you, Daniele, must promise you will come back tomorrow morning to make a last goodbye.'

'Of course I shall come back.'

'Perhaps I had better go with you, Zelda,' said her mother when she was already at the door. '*Ma pauvre chérie*, it's not fair that it's always you who has to see to everything: I want to make myself useful too, for once. See you tomorrow then, Mr Bausa; see you later, Rasmi.'

We remained alone, and Stiler turned to look at me. He seemed exhausted, as if he had been obliged to exert a strenuous self-control for too long.

'I,' I began falteringly, 'don't really know what to say.'

'Then don't say anything, Bausa, there's no need to talk about it.'

He went over to the piano, which Zelda had left open, and slowly lowered the lid.

'If my being here makes things awkward for you, engineer . . .'

'On the contrary, dear friend, I shall be happy if you would stay a bit longer. Only, would you mind coming into the garden with me?'

'I'll go with you gladly.'

We went outside. The oak tree had been removed and in its place a large circular pit gaped open.

'You see, Bausa? I finally got around to it.'

'Ah, yes. And now what do you plan to do?'

He gave me an intense, penetrating look. 'I shall plant another oak tree: I've already ordered a sapling. Of course I won't be able to see it fully grown like its partner, it takes years, but this partial defeat ought to satisfy your aesthetic sense.'

I followed him as he inspected the garden inch by inch, with a critical eye, listing the kinds of work that were necessary to restore its former appearance. At last we reached Artemis's flower-bed and he walked into it, stepping between the sods of loose earth. Suddenly I saw him bend down: he had found a red flower, one which had survived the destruction wreaked upon the big Z. He picked it and stood staring at it with a look of absorption; for a little while as we walked along the path together, he kept rolling it absent-mindedly between his fingers, as if he meant to throw it away from one moment to the next, but when he thought himself unobserved he quickly slipped it into one of his jacket pockets.

The following morning, the garden was enveloped in dampness, halfway between fog and a fine drizzle, from which the outlines of the hedges and flower-beds emerged faint and misty. I had made my way to the villa very early, as agreed, so that I could make a leisurely leavetaking with the ladies, but when I arrived Zee's automobile was already outside the door. She and her mother stood waiting in the hallway, while Stiler nervously looked over the luggage.

'Are you sure you haven't forgotten anything?'

'Quite sure, Rasmi,' replied the aunt.

'This suitcase isn't properly closed... There, it's all right now. All we're waiting for is the gardener if he will deign to come and fetch the luggage.'

I could be in no doubt that this separation caused him pain, and yet he seemed actually impatient to see it done with: perhaps out of some defensive instinct, he was concentrating all of his attention on the departure, attempting to reduce it to a series of operations to be carried out in the most rational way and with absolute promptness. Zee too seemed ill at ease, and my arrival evidently gave her some relief.

'Have you seen the weather, Daniele? This place is really keen to make us leave. Anyway it's better like this, I wouldn't have liked to go off on a sunny morning.'

'From now on sunny mornings will be increasingly rare. I'll soon have to go back to town too.'

'And poor Rasmi,' said the aunt in a pitying tone, 'will be staying here all alone, buried in the fog.'

'In the fog and in the snow,' the engineer amended. 'In a couple of months the garden will be entirely white, and the access road will freeze over.'

Zee looked him straight in the eyes, but said nothing. At that moment Ursula's husband came in to fetch the luggage.

'Mind now, the two biggest ones at the back of the car boot,' said Stiler.

The man went outside and closed the door after him, and a tense silence fell among us. A very faint glimmering was shed through the windows of the adjoining rooms, but no one had thought to turn on the light: that penumbra, in which our expressions became indecipherable, was greeted with unspoken gratitude. The walls and furniture too were scarcely visible, and for a moment I imagined I stood once again in the house as it had appeared the first time I saw it, with neither ceilings nor partition walls, resembling a disused church.

When the gardener returned to announce that the car was ready, Stiler went up to his cousin. 'I shall really miss you, Zelda.'

'Yes, Erasmo, you already said so.'

'I wanted to tell you again.'

'The time for these things is over, we're leaving now. Dear Daniele, it has been a pleasure to know you.'

'The pleasure has been mine. Madam, I bid you goodbye.'

'See you soon, Mr Bausa. We're counting on a visit from you when you are in town.'

Stiler turned to his aunt and kissed her quickly on

both cheeks; he hesitated momentarily before doing the same with Zee. 'We'll write, I suppose.'

'Certainly, we'll write.'

Holding the umbrella, he saw his aunt, then his cousin, to the car. I stayed on the threshold watching. There were no other embraces between them, and as the engine took its time revving up, Stiler came back beside me.

'It will be a very long winter, Bausa.'

✥ EPILOGUE ✥

LITTLE BY LITTLE the life of the villa re-assumed its habitual progress, while Zee and her troubling influence became ever more remote, confined to the faded realm of memories. Very soon the garden showed once again the most total submission to the will of its creator, and Artemis, finally appeased by the sacrifice carried out by Stiler, cast a benevolent gaze down upon us from her pedestal. The only sign that still revealed the upheaval we had witnessed was the young oak tree planted in the place of the one that had been felled and which was disproportionately small in relation to its ancient partner on the other side of the avenue; but Stiler, strange to say, did not seem at all put out by that disharmony, perhaps because he saw it as the indispensable premiss for a future harmony.

The young oak tree grew slowly, year by year, and meanwhile I continued to come and go regularly between the city and the village with the changing seasons. When my university studies were over I had chosen teaching as a profession, without this choice being prompted by any particular vocation: I had simply opted for a career which assured me abundant free time, the possibility of carrying on with my painting, and above all very long holidays. Moreover, it was a profession, at least as I understood it, which seemed made for me, since it consisted in preparing others for something which I personally took care not to engage with.

As soon as the school year was over I would therefore leave for the village, look out through the window of my usual train at the slow alteration of the landscape, take up lodging in the usual room where the year before I had made sure to leave behind some object or garment, and the following morning set out towards Stiler's abode. I was always impatient to see him again and I knew that he awaited me with equal impatience. He had frequently even offered me hospitality in his home, but I preferred our friendship to preserve that hint of distance and mutual reserve with which it had been marked from the start; nor, I am sure, would Stiler willingly have given it up. For the same reason we maintained the same formalities of speech; yet, the more time passed and I became aware that I would not readily abandon my stance as observer, between us, despite our extremely different characters, there became ever firmer the silent alliance of those who have turned their backs on life, and it mattered little that my renunciation had its origins in indolence, whereas his came from an ardent and active ambition.

One might say that by now Stiler had in me his only link with the world; he had never again left his property except to go down to the village, whose inhabitants welcomed him with the deference due to a man who had been able to resist the irresistible temptation represented by Zee; they also esteemed the new serenity of his demeanour, the tranquil manners he had assumed ever since he had definitively acknowledged himself as a master of chance, but familiarity of any kind was avoided most rigorously by both parties, and Stiler's contacts with the local people continued to take the form of curt questions and curt answers.

No more little chicken bones ever came to disturb his routines as a hard-working hermit and no one bothered to release the automobile, long since reduced to a pile of scrap iron, from the tight embrace in which the creepers held it. It had now become a natural element, a strange bush which poked out from the garden's perimeter wall, and Stiler seemed actually to take pleasure in its state of dereliction, perhaps discerning in it a material symbol of his own irremovability.

An unacknowledged law always governed our conversations, forbidding us from uttering Zee's name or alluding in any way to that business. Her memory had to be treated with caution, like a wound which had not completely healed, a faint but persistent ache.

The year following his separation from his cousin, Stiler had taken me, on my return, before the statue of Artemis, and without a word had shown me the big Z of red blooms which once more stood out against the green of the flower-bed. From then on he replanted it each spring, repeating his gesture of mute fidelity with the same diligence with which a religious ceremony is celebrated on the dates and in the forms established once and for all by the liturgy. He had also kept the piano, which remained in the drawing-room, forever closed, untouched by any hand.

The regard in which I held him did not prevent me from wondering whether his actions might in reality be dictated by fear, by a secret dismay in the face of that nothingness into which our each and every striving is doomed to sink. Perhaps the precision of his projects was an attempt to hold that force in check, to elude it, and the order which he had constructed and strenuously defended in the garden served to hide from his own eyes the absurd truth of annihilation.

Sometimes I even suspected that there was more courage in my way of living, observing the course of events without trying to set myself against their senselessness. Certainly, as Stiler would have said, adopting such a line of conduct meant removing oneself from everything entailed in the proper task of a rational being, embracing the ethic of the octopus and the crayfish, giving oneself over to a philosophy so inclined to logical and moral laxity that it even refused to effect any clear distinction between God and nothing.

And yet in Stiler's proclaimed ban on little chicken bones there was something which brought to my mind the complicated exorcisms of savages to keep hostile demons at bay. His cosmos was a cunning exception trimmed out of chaos, and the latter laid siege to him on all sides in the same way that the hills laid siege to the geometry of the garden with their untamed vegetation. Therein resided the charm of Stiler's enterprise, and simultaneously its weakness: I grieved for him whenever I remembered how much he had sacrificed to his own fear despite his awareness that sooner or later nothingness would prevail in the end; I grieved whenever I saw him lavish every attention on the young oak tree whose full development he would never look upon, and when I saw him behave in whatever circumstance as if he had been granted immortality.

He was bound to everything that surrounded him by

a chain so solid with duties and tasks that at any moment whatsoever his death would amount to a catastrophe; I, on the other hand, always had my bags packed, I inhabited life with the same sense of the provisional and the same lack of obligations with which one takes a room in a hotel, and often, comparing my fate with that of the engineer, I told myself that for me the departure would be a much smoother one.

But whatever his expectations were, the engineer had not been vouchsafed immortality. From being an abstract perception, this truth appeared to me as a concrete threat when Stiler began to turn into an old man, when his hair whitened and a dense network of wrinkles was overlaid on his face. With each year that passed, such changes were made obvious to me by the long separations, which prevented routine from masking them, and every time I went back to the village at the end of the winter I found myself faced with new devastations wreaked by time upon the person of Erasmo Stiler.

Yet old age had not managed to bend his back, still erect like that of a young man, nor had it diminished his energy, which was wholly devoted to the garden. He worked zealously, every day, spending hours outdoors even at the coldest times of year, and if it rained you could see his gaunt figure hurrying from one part of the property to another under the shelter of a wide oilskin cape. The waning of physical strength was almost imperceptible in him, so much did he make up for it with a doggedness that actually seemed to draw fresh sustenance from age, and it was certainly because of this doggedness, more than from any particular vigour, that one would never find the engineer ill.

I discovered too late how deceptive was that display of good health: I discovered it abruptly, cruelly, without being prepared by any warning sign; on the contrary, by then I was convincing myself that Erasmo Stiler would have the privilege of an altogether special old age, one immune from all insults, one long and majestic like that of the sempiternal oak. With this conviction I had left him to return to the city, one late September morning, and as I went out through the gate of the villa I had not looked back.

In January I was reached at my apartment by a halting telegram in which Ursula informed me that the engineer was seriously ill, and she begged me to waste no time in getting there. I left that same day, but I did not arrive in time to say goodbye to my friend: while I was on the train bronchial pneumonia had finally succeeded in dragging him away from the garden.

Ursula and I spent the night keeping watch. The stiffness of his body in death was so little different from that stiffness he had always preserved when he was alive, that from one moment to the next I expected to see him sit up and leap out of bed in a start of impatience.

Not even in that dire situation did Ursula give up complaining about her master: she reproached him with having died out of pure and simple stubbornness, taking it into his head to be up and about and to go outside, despite having that cold, so as not to neglect his tasks. To the very end he had even refused to call the doctor, perhaps because in his heart he knew that the man would have ordered him to stay in bed, as moreover Ursula had been advising him to do for the last week.

'Yes, sir, the doctor would have said I was right and he was wrong. And the dear departed, as you well know, would not have admitted he was wrong for anything in the world: better to die, instead, and go on insisting so long as he still had a breath, that I was a fearful and interfering little woman, that I should mind my own business, that he could look after himself . . . In fact, now we see.'

From time to time she would break off to blow her nose and dry fat tears that streamed down her cheeks. I was not weeping, but I had the sensation that from that day on my baggage had become even lighter.

'We shall need to let the relatives know.'

'I have already seen to it, sir; shortly before you arrived I went down to the village and I telegraphed Miss Zelda. Think of it, she was still in the engineer's address book, her old address and the new one underneath it, where she lives now, with a whole page to herself. It's true that he couldn't have known many people whose name began with Z, but it's touching all the same. She'll be upset about it, poor thing, even though she hadn't seen him in years.'

I looked around that cold, unadorned room, and it struck me that all of it would have been less sad, or at any rate with a sadness that was different and more human, if instead of the aged Ursula sitting by the dead man's bedside, there had been Zee in elegant widow's weeds, and beside her maybe some boy in whose features, in whose gestures and demeanour I could have glimpsed an unconscious repetition of Stiler's physiognomy. Then perhaps I would not have felt that sense of desolation, of total futility, perhaps the continuity of life would have spread its reassuring veil over that body, concealing its loneliness. And yet Stiler had preferred the severe mourning of the snow-covered garden to all of that.

Zelda did not come to her cousin's funeral; together with her mother and a husband of whose existence I knew nothing up until that moment, she published a death notice in a newspaper, and no more. Her absence could be justified by the distance of the city where she now lived, and the advanced age of her mother, who doubtless needed constant care, but I suspected that the true reason for it was a tenacious rancour, unattenuated by the passing of the years. As for the numerous company of aunts and uncles, male and female cousins who once used to gather round the Christmas tree and together open presents wrapped in brightly coloured paper, neither then nor later was anything heard of them.

The burial was dispatched with no time wasted and, in accordance with the wish repeatedly expressed by the engineer himself, without any religious ceremony. Compelled by circumstances to assume the role which would have fallen to a close relative, I had had the coffin brought out to the garden, in front of the big flower-bed, so that my friend could take his leave of Artemis. Here, as the goddess looked down, I would have liked to make a commemorative speech in honour of Stiler, had there been anyone to hear it; but the audience was made up only of Ursula, the gardener and the undertaker's men, so I remained silent, and after a few minutes I ordered the pall bearers to lift the bier and load it onto the funeral carriage parked in front of the house.

The black vehicle crossed the expanse of snow beneath which the garden pondered its blossoming into spring, for the sight of unknown eyes; when it had disappeared through the gate I set out for the cemetery, accompanied by the two servants.

'What killed him, sir,' Ursula said, casting glances of superstitious hostility all around her, 'was this place and no mistake.'

'In that case,' I retorted, 'the engineer died of what he had lived by.'

As we went down the avenue it began snowing again in sparse flakes, and on reaching the village I found it more silent and deserted than I had ever seen. The snow muffled sound, and reabsorbed every trace of human actions into its slow movement. Even the deep ruts ploughed by the wheels of the funeral carriage would be erased almost at once by that white indifference.

In front of the cemetery a group of locals waited for us, among whom I recognised the most faithful of the café regulars. They stood to one side, and also kept some distance following the coffin, as if they were uncertain whether what was happening really was to do with them. When the bier was lowered into the ground they made the sign of the cross and the men took off their berets, but a moment later they put them on again as protection from the snow. Then, without waiting for the grave to be closed over, the group dispersed.

I thought that after Stiler's death I would have stopped my visits to the village forever, but I went there a few months later. I could scarcely believe that the garden had awakened from its winter somnolence as if nothing had happened, and even the return of spring suddenly struck me as an absurd occurrence, since not one flower, not a single blade of grass from those that had lived the previous year would have returned.

As soon as I arrived I realised that spring paid no attention to such trivialities, nor did the garden seem willing to wear mourning for the death of its former master. Everything grew, burgeoned, turned green in a state of insolent exultation. Artemis watched over the tender grass of the flower-bed with self-satisfied majesty, and the ghastly forgetfulness of these creatures aroused in me simultaneous feelings of indignation and envy.

I hadn't had any trouble getting in, because no one had bothered to lock the gate. I knew that the villa was uninhabited: Zee had inherited it from her cousin, but she had never come nor had she given any instructions about it. I headed for Ursula's cottage, but I found the doors and windows bolted, and on the outside, where the roses had been, a bare skeleton of branches. Only the plaster gnomes, the gaudy lustre of their colours still unaltered, maintained a comical substitute for some human presence. In the village I asked for news of the two servants and was told that they had moved elsewhere.

The following year the situation appeared unchanged, but in that dereliction the garden began to display a wilder vitality, a lack of restraint which no one now took care to correct. The creepers had triumphantly reconquered the walls of the villa, the flower-beds, unconfined, had lost their geometric shapes, and in place of the highly bred species cultivated by Stiler there burgeoned wildflowers whose seeds must have been borne inside the property's boundaries by the wind. The birds, in great numbers, sang full-throatedly in this place once cloaked in silence; of all the foliage, they displayed a distinct predilection for the two oak trees, and some had built nests in their branches.

It was obvious that the garden was shaking off the yoke imposed by Stiler for so long, and it did so, year after year, with astonishing rapidity, as if rushing to erase any memory of its former subjection. The engineer's heir, to all appearances, had no intention of living in the villa, but nor was she inclined to sell it, and it was precisely this aversion which had seen to it that her marble twin had changed colour, covering herself from head to toe in a layer of moss. Assuming, I thought sometimes, that behind this shilly-shallying which condemned the garden to desolation, Zee was not hiding some unconscious yearning for vengeance.

Thus, year after year, Erasmo Stiler died, in a sense which seemed to me more fundamental, more terrible than his own physical death. What died was his will, his ambition, that challenge which he had laid down to the forces of chaos, carrying off a victory whose illusory nature was only now fully disclosed to me. And I looked on at every phase of this death, continuing to visit the garden, or what was left of it, with a peculiar tenacity. Perhaps I meant to keep faith to the very last with my role as witness, even though I was conscious that in the end nothingness would get the better of this testimony, as with its object; but Erasmo Stiler had

taught me to grasp the grandeur of hopeless undertakings, and I was sure, am sure, that had he been able
to foresee the outcome of his efforts, had he been
able to observe that ruination, he would have acted in
exactly the same way, despite everything. While
knowing the invincible power of dissolution, he would
have chosen to conduct his own life as if some eternal
trace of it were destined to remain: any other decision,
however wise, would have seemed to him unworthy of
a man. I would have said all this, that day beside Stiler's
coffin, if there had been anyone there who could have
listened to me.

With the passage of time the village kept on growing,
expanding towards the valley, and the customers at the
café, which had turned into a modern bar with high
plastic-covered stools and a profusion of chrome fit-
tings, no longer even turned to look now as numerous
cars went by. So I stopped spending my summers there
and sought out more distant country areas, landscapes
uncorroded by the slow canker which the city where I
live seems to spread around itself, but these days I still
go back there at least once a year to complete a pil-
grimage to what was the garden. I feel that I could not
really honour the memory of the engineer without at
the same time honouring his adversary, the force by
which he was vanquished. For this reason I never go
to the cemetery, and it doesn't bother me to know that
no one takes flowers to Stiler's grave. If any funeral
monument exists to which his memory is entrusted, it
is to be found up there, behind the derelict house: it is
a moss-covered statue, which still casts its firm gaze

down from its pedestal upon the expanse of weeds with which it is surrounded.

Every year I set out towards that destination, making my way with difficulty along the asphalt road, which is now flanked by an array of snow-white villas, and when I reach the rusty gate I discern a tangle of vegetation in which it is hard for me to recognise the place where Erasmo Stiler had constructed his symmetries. Nature's asymmetry has overpowered them by now, and every time, after rendering my homage to Artemis, I stay there for hours contemplating the peculiar hybrids produced by the conjunction of two opposing laws, as I make quick sketches in my album and then immediately cross them out. I finally close my album again and go off disheartened, despairing of ever being able to draw that garden, of ever recreating its gloomy fascination on paper.

Also by Paola Capriolo and published by Serpent's Tail

Floria Tosca
Translated by Liz Heron

Based on Puccini's opera, *Floria Tosca* reinterprets for today's times the relationship between Scarpia, chief of police, and Tosca, singer and lover of Cavaradossi, the radical, whom Scarpia plans to arrest and torture. In elegant, precise writing, Paola Capriolo takes us to a world where love and hatred, piety and devilry, abstinence and desire come together.

'Elegant, cunning and cruel, *Floria Tosca* will appeal to any opera lover who finds the virtuous heroes of the form crashing bores compared with their godless counterparts' Patrick Gale

'The mechanics and pleasures of the meeting between sadist and masochist have rarely been so elegantly handled as in the story of Tosca ... Paola Capriolo has given a new, nasty, elaborately mannered and highly entertaining twist to the classic tale of fatal attraction of policeman for diva. I suggest you put on the Callas recording, pour yourself a drink, turn the lights down, read, and surrender' Neil Bartlett

'Brilliant ... Heron's translation manages to be both artful and absorbing ... it compels the recognition that very little in the English-language Gothic tradition can compare with the sheer intellectual sophistication of Paola Capriolo's novel' *New York Times Book Review*

'An exhilarating tale of fatal attraction' *Good Book Guide*

The Woman Watching
Translated by Liz Heron

What is the nature of the actor's mask? At what point do performer and performance merge? Vulpius, a much admired young actor in a provincial rep company, develops an obsession with an unknown spectator whose gaze seems only for him, at first kindling fresh fervour in his mastery of each role, then leaving him a slave to artistic perfection.

With philosophical elegance and black macabre sense of comedy, Paola Capriolo draws the reader deep into obsession, exploring the most compelling recesses of the theatrical experience where ritual and stylisation run rampant. Dark questions emerge about the power of representation and the dangers of sacrificing life to art. *The Woman Watching* is a work of art at the very centre of European literary culture: a culture it wears lightly and with elegance.

'Capriolo's forte is the exquisite philosophical game played with corrosive scepticism' *TLS*

'The dangers of art are part of what art is. Both as novelist and essayist Capriolo has no doubt about the validity of fictional ironies and artificialities. In this novel she achieves a new lucidity in her juxtaposition of mirroring looks and in her playing of construction and deconstruction against each other' *New York Times Book Review*

'This is the kind of intellectually elegant book that we just do not seem to write on this side of the channel' *Sunday Times*